# Threads of Fate

A Paranormal Interracial Erotic Romance

**Lexi Esme**

# Contents

# Rhianne

I lean my head against the window of Gary's sleek black Mercedes and look at the passing scenery. It's a dark cloudy night, the windows are dotted with the beginnings of an autumnal shower, and my guilt is eating me alive.

"Looks like there's a storm coming," I say, breaking the silence.

"Yup," Gary says, he turns on the wipers, and they swipe at the sparse droplets on the windshield.

I hear the distant crack of thunder, and quickly say, "I don't like thunderstorms."

I shift in my seat to face him. "I'm really sorry about this, Mr. Edwards," I begin. "I could've gotten a taxi or used a ride share app–you didn't have to go through the trouble–"

"Rhianne, really, it's fine. How were you to know that your car would break down outside in the parking lot?" he says. He raises his thick salt and pepper eyebrows and smiles at me.

"Yeah, but I feel so bad. We've been at work for almost ten hours, and now you have to take me home."

"Eh, what's another hour of civic duty?" he says, smirking.

I sigh, and Gary pats my hand. "I'm only teasing. Really, Rhianne, it's fine. After hours, we're not just boss and employee; we're friends. Friends take care of friends. Isn't that your motto? Speaking of, I told you a hundred times to call me Gary."

"You're right. Sorry Mr.–," I quickly correct myself with a bashful smile, "I mean, Gary,"

He laughs again, and I relax a little more into my seat.

I refocus my sights on the view outside. The city's lights slowly drown out, and all I can see are tall trees and twists of the road beyond the raindrops on the windows. The rain begins to come down with a vengeance, growing faster and more relentless with each passing second and the wipers fight desperately to keep up.

There's barely anyone else on the road, and as we continue, I notice that signage grows few and far between. I look down at my hands, folded neatly in my lap, wring them together, then give the dashboard clock another glance. It's only eight-thirty.

I shouldn't feel this anxious, and yet, I do. I lick my lips and glance at Gary.

"Uh, Gary," I venture hesitantly, my voice just above the tinny pattering of rain against the car roof. Gary glances at me quickly in the rearview mirror, and then his eyes fall back on the road ahead.

"This isn't the way to my house." I go on, a little more sharply now. "Maybe you should turn on the GPS. I don't want you to get lost."

Gary snorts. "Relax. This is a shortcut. I take this way all the time to get to your home."

I furrow my brows, trying to think back to the last time I invited him over. I can't dredge up a memory of it.

"I'm sorry, when have you been to my house?"

His silence makes the short hairs on the back of my neck stand.

"When have you been to my house?" I repeat.

He only continues to stare forward. "Do you remember when you came to *Visionaries* to work for me?" He asks offhandedly, catching me off-guard. "I do. It was one of the best days of my life. You were so impressive during your interview. I knew I was going to hire you. And over the years, I never once regretted the decision. Not once."

I watch as the number on the speedometer increases from forty miles per hour to sixty. The click of the locks makes me jump in my seat, and I suddenly feel claustrophobic. I can't find any words to say, so I keep quiet. Gary doesn't seem to notice, because he keeps on without pause.

"It didn't take long for me to fall madly in love with you." He chuckled harshly. "And you *rejected* me."

"I don't date people I work with. It's a rule of mine...Besides, you're my boss, and I'm not comfortable with that." I wonder what happened to the traffic. I search the other lanes, but they're empty.

"Rhianne, I never once questioned your rejection until you flirted with me."

"I've never flirted with you." I try to keep my indignation— and disgust— out of my tone.

He turns and faces me. The gray of his eyes is so dark they make him look soulless. "Two years ago, April 17th, you *complimented* me on my tie. Your exact words were, 'Good pick. It goes well with your suit.' One year ago, July 24th, you called me Gary for the first time." He closes his eyes, causing the car to swerve slightly. "The way it rolled from your lips left me hard all day..."

A shiver goes down my spine. I open my mouth to say something, but I'm so flabbergasted I shut it again. Did he just say what I think he said?

"...From then on, I knew you were mine, and I always protect what is mine. I followed you home every day to make sure you were safe...and alone." His thin lips curl into a smile that makes my stomach drop. "You knew I was there. I know you did. That's why you always undress in front of the window, behind that sheer curtain. You *wanted* me to see that perfect body of yours."

His hand reaches out tremblingly before he rests it on my thigh giving it a squeeze, I jerk away from him, but he only grips tighter. "Tinkering with your car was my play in our game, but how about we skip the song and dance we've been doing for two years and get to the point? Things have gotten dicey at work, and we need to get out of town for a bit."

"I'm not going anywhere with you— " I gasp. "Don't do this. If you take me home right now, I promise all is forgiven. I won't tell anyone. We can just go back to how things were."

"But don't you get it? I want you to tell. I want you to tell the world how good I made you feel. I want you to show them you're mine." He yanks the wheel to the right, and the car careens from the road.

Slamming his foot on the brake pedal, he halts the car a mere moment before it collides into a tree. All I can hear is the sound of the rain and the beating of my own heart. In the seclusion of the woods, he unbuckles his seatbelt and faces me. Meanwhile, I pull feverishly at the door handle.

"Knock it off!" he screams, reaching for me.

I swat at his beefy hands, but he easily catches my wrist, yanking me across the seat. "Stop, Gary! Please!— " Recoiling from him, I try to twist out of his grip.

"I said fucking knock it off!" he shouts, drawing his hand back.

The sting of his slap sends my face snapping to the side, and my head rings. And for a moment, everything in me is frozen, and my brain can't form a single coherent thought. I can taste the coppery tang of blood, I feel it pooling from my nose. Tears fill my eyes, but I blink them away.

"You think you're better than me, huh? You think I don't deserve you? I *made* you. You are nothing without me. Maybe you need a reminder of that."

He unlocks the door and rushes to the passenger side before I can react, and he wrenches my door open, pulling me out by my hair into the rainy night.

I try to claw my way away from him, but he throws me onto the sodden earth. My head slams against a stone, and the world around me seems to fade.

"Rhianne?"

His words are muffled, and he swims in my vision, I can barely make out his expression.

"Rhianne?!" Gary's hands fly to his mouth, and he fumbles to find my pulse. I feel myself fading, but I fight it.

"Rhi-ahhh!— "

It takes nearly all my strength, but my foot connects squarely with his groin, and I watch him crumple over.

"You bitch!" Gary rasps, holding his crotch.

I scramble to my feet, but in my disorientation, the entire world moves in a crooked circle. I stagger forward and fall on my hands and knees onto wet leaves, dirt and gravel, but I use them as leverage to push myself up to my feet once again. Thoroughly drenched and covered in dirt, I take off into the blackened woods.

"Help!" I plead as I draw further into the darkness. Leaves crunching behind me tell me Gary isn't far behind, and he laughs wildly in pursuit.

"I love this new game!"

My heart is pounding out of my chest, and my lungs burn with every breath I take, but I can't stop. My feet splashing in the puddles, I race deeper into the woods.

All at once, a flash of lightning illuminates the forest like a camera flash; the trees become stark silhouettes against a dreary sky.

“Help! Please, help!” The sound of my yelling is swallowed by the heavy rain, whipping wind, and the bone-rattling boom of thunder.

Gary's footfalls are moments away now, and I can almost feel his breath on my neck.

*Please...someone...please help.*

I think a silent prayer to myself, but I'm not sure to who. Just as Gary's hand grabs a fistful of my hair, I feel my feet lose purchase of the ground beneath me; it loosens and splits, crumbling beneath my feet like it's made of sand.

Before I know it, I'm tumbling down, with Gary following after.

My heart in my throat, I scream. My arms flail wildly as I try to find something to grab onto, but I slam painfully into the ground hard on my back, the air driven from my lungs. Crashing into the ground, it’s every bit as painful as I imagined. I cringe and suck in my breath, my body racked with pain.

A loud bang follows, just inches from me, as Gary falls into the pit shortly after. He doesn't move.

I’m sprawled on the ground, gasping for air. To lay down, and not get up might be the kindest thing to do, but I know I'm not quite out of the woods yet.

"Gary?" I say, my voice emerges from my throat hoarse and pained.

No answer comes.

"Gary?" I try again.

Nothing.

Trying to adjust to the darkness, I blink several times, squeezing my eyes shut. I drag myself up from the ground as quickly as my aching body will allow. I strive to see in the pitch blackness of the place, but as the clouds shift overhead, a soft ray of moonlight allows me to make out a dirt-covered wall beside me.

I look down at myself. I'm covered in wet dirt, my clothes torn, and bloodied. My entire body aches from the fall, but I'm alive.

Just as quickly the clouds converge like a curtain dropping on a stage. All is in darkness again. I can't make out most of my surroundings, but it seems we've landed in a pit. It's relatively drier down here; the air hangs damply, heavily, thick with the smell of earth and nitrates.

My hands grope blindly along the walls of the place to find a steady foothold, a rock, a vine, anything. My searching fingers soon discover something hard and curved, and I smirk imagining it to be a tree root. Grabbing hold, I test some of my weight on it, but it shifts in the dirt wall, causing me to lose balance. I stagger back from it but my hand comes away sticky and with much effort.

Wonderingly, and still half dazed, I open and close my hand, feeling a clinging substance reluctantly stretching between my fingers as I pry them apart, almost like stretchy sap-covered hairs or vines. I wonder at what I just touched, I try to wipe my hand clean against my torn pencil skirt, and it very nearly adheres. I'm forced to rip my hand back, with a shuddering breath.

Something feels so wrong about this place, and I begin to wonder where I am in earnest, and as though in answer, there is a sudden and momentary flash of lightning. For a moment, I can make out the walls that surround me, and ice pours through my veins...

"Oh my God."

The pit extends far beyond, and behind me and Gary, far above us too, but what lines the pit is truly horrifying:

Shredded clothing. Bones. Disturbingly familiar-looking shapes, swathed, cocooned, in thick layers of a fine white fabric substance. And lacing the walls, miles of silvery threads.

*Spiderwebs?*

Recognizing the impossible material, I want to scream. Nothing comes out.

Worse still, a sound carries in the darkness just a few short feet away.

"Fuck..."

It's almost a relief to hear that it's only Gary. I can just barely make him out, struggling to sit up.

Gary groans in pain. Finally, having come to, his silhouette rises to his feet. I hear a jangling of car keys before a thin beam of yellow light cuts through the darkness. For an instant, I'm grateful Gary is here until I remember he just assaulted me and likely has plans for worse.

I back away several steps and away from the light, my hands raised to shield my eyes.

"Rhianne?...Well, at the very least, I still have you here with me...it looks like I haven't lost everything. I would have taken you with me, Rhianne, we could've lived a beautiful life together, but you don't seem to want that, which means I'll have no use for you after tonight. At the very least, this is the perfect place to leave you to rot if you continue to disrespect me."

*Damn it. I guess not even circumstances can change Gary's priorities.*

I retreat a fair distance from him before he redirects the beam of light elsewhere. He shines the mini flashlight along the walls, lingering on what I've just witnessed but not quite understanding what he sees. I can see it in the faint light; his hand is shaking.

"Where am-" But Gary's sentence breaks as yet another noise whispers through the darkness, a faint crackling. Following the sound with his flashlight, the beam lands at a far corner, where something shadowy quickly slips from view.

"Christ!" The flashlight drops from his hands, made clumsy in his fear. Keys and all fall to the ground in a cacophony of jingling; and all is lost to darkness once again.

"What was that?" I whisper in a harsh breath, wondering if I'd seen anything at all.

“Shit...shit!” Is all Gary says, fumbling around for his keys.

And then we both see it.

Red eyes peer back at us from the abyssal dark, and contortions of bone fill the night air.

Gary stumbles backward, and keen, rubied eyes follow his every movement.

The next part happens in slow motion, as though in a nightmare.

I watch as an enormous long pointed appendage amasses from the darkness. Black and lacquered, reflecting the faintest moonlight, it plants itself firmly in the earth.

Gary is staggering back, his heel accidentally kicking the car keys; they skitter, then bounce off into the darkness, lost.

Several uneven shafts of moonlight reveal the scene unfold before me. Gary’s eyes bulge at the sight of the other. He can’t speak. He can only watch as the creature reveals more of itself. The sight of another black leg, and then another, make his face lose all color. He turns and locks eyes with me, the fear on his face making my own double.

He opens his mouth, but no words rise from his throat. Instead, a loud gargle pierces the silence. I feel a scattered spatter of warm liquid across my face and clothing, and I damn near hyperventilate.

Shakingly, Gary looks down at his chest. Velvet blood pools and stains the ground as the creature’s leg twists inside of him. It pulls Gary from his feet and brings him several feet into the air.

Blood pours from his open mouth, and he wraps his fists around the wrist-thick, serrated appendage that holds him impaled and suspended, to no avail. His grip slips off the creature like it's coated in oil.

"H-help me," he chokes out to me, twisting towards me in the creature's hold, but I can only sink to my knees, my legs having lost all feeling.

Gary is easily pulled towards the creature, toward the dark body that seems to absorb all of the light. It lashes band after band of silk webbing around him, the shiny threads glistening like silver stripes in the otherwise steady tapestry of shadows and darkness. Gary's legs kick spastically in the air, but hauntingly, the creature runs another dark appendage down Gary's horrified face in a final caress.

Its almost calm, deep growl comes back to me: "Hush, be silent now."

I watch on, horrified.

It lifts him higher, twining the fine threads in a wide sheet around and around his legs, working quickly to cocoon him compactly, like its victims in the walls. And sickeningly, I hear hollow cracking sounds, like a branch snapping in half, as the creature twists and pulls and tightens, seemingly only finding the fruitless struggles of its food amusing. The flailing Gary screams as bones are broken, but the sound is soon choked back down his throat. Gary's screams are silenced in an instant. The creature quickly wraps the last of the silky substance over his head, then continues to envelop him until he is silent. until he is still.

Gary's tightly cocooned form is hoisted on a silken rope, slung up, and secured in a high corner.

Sick to my stomach, my gaze lowers to my hand, covered in the unknown substance but now also dotted with dark blood, realizing it is the very same substance Gary is enshrouded in. I can't get the image of Gary's face, his cries, the sound of his breaking bones, out of my head.

And now the creature approaches, its slow and heavy footfalls sounding out as it turns, like it's looking to me, as though noticing me for the very first time.

In a blind panic, I turn away from the horror of the thing before me and begin to crawl on all fours. I don't see a way out, and I don't know where I am going, I just go.

Time slows.

I don't want to look up and face the creature that I know scales the walls above me. Quaking, I lift my head, my scream is amplified by the walls around me as it lunges directly at me.

# Rhianne

Encased in the darkness, I shut my eyes tightly and hear the heavy thud of the creature land in front of me, blocking my path. I wait for the singe of its fangs, or the pierce of its leg to sink into my flesh as it did Gary. I cringe against the cool bare earth of the pit.

"You shouldn't be here..."

He? It definitely sounds like a he, speaks again, and there's something almost elegant in his voice, a slight accent, barely noticeable, that I cannot place.

*No —fucking— duh, I shouldn't be here.*

I'm so terrified my voice won't come at all, but after several attempts, I eventually manage: "L-Let me go, please..." I can't hold back my shudder as the words finally break free from my lips.

The creature doesn't answer for a time. Finally, it responds: "What is your name?"

I raise my head but can't make myself open my eyes to face the enormous monster in front of me.

I open my mouth to answer, but the only thing that comes out is a choked sob. Trying again, I stammer: "R-Rhianne...please, I– "

The creature doesn't even allow me the chance to beg for my life, it simply says back, voice soft: "Rhianne? A pretty name." My name sounds almost like a caress on its lips, and it is silent once again.

*For a pretty meal, I suppose.*

I don't dare voice the thought aloud, I don't say anything. It takes a step closer and my lungs seize, my thoughts scatter like leaves in a storm. I can only kneel in fear while its silhouette towers over me, so much so that I am forced to squeeze my eyes shut and face my knees.

"A-are you going to eat– ?" I can't bear to finish the sentence. My breath rushes out in a silent scream as the creature's leg jabs into the ground next to me and draws nearer, scraping along the dirt and stone ground.

"Should I eat you?" He sounds almost amused.

I shake my head desperately. "But, you're a monster– and I thought-"

A deep exhale drifts down from above me, and I open my eyes. It's still too dark to make out his features, silhouetted and still mostly lost to shadow. I can only see that he towers above me (whether I'm sitting or standing), his hulking body, and spider-like appendages surrounding me like a cage.

"A monster..." He chuckles, and the sound is hollow. I detect something thoughtful, but also sad in his tone and guilt hits me instantly. "It is not the first time I've been given that name. I have no plans to harm you. Interestingly enough, from your screams earlier, I doubt I am the only monster you've encountered tonight."

My eyes travel to the dark wet patch of dirt where the earth has drunk deep of Gary's blood. Did he think he had saved me? Then again, I suppose he has.

"D-Do *you* have a name?" I ask, now unsure of what to say.

"Me?" His tone is almost one of surprise, and a low rumble of laughter follows. "I suppose I have many names, among them 'Monster'."

"I'm sorry– I shouldn't have said that–" My face burns with chagrin, but then I wonder why I should feel this way at all.

"No need to be...I don't blame you. Under these circumstances and most any other, to you, I would seem quite...monstrous." He pauses. "I am called Sephtis..."

"Sephtis?" I repeat, from far above me, I sense he gives a nod, and the faintly red glow of his eyes dances. I then realize how utterly stupid it is of me to be doing this. I'm talking to a giant, man-eating spider-being in a pit, with absolutely no means of escape.

*He claims he doesn't plan to hurt me.* I reason. *Gary claimed to want to help me...he didn't have the intention of hurting me either. Until he did, and planned on hurting me far worse...*

"If we are done with the pleasantries, I would like for you to leave, Rhianne." The lacquered foreleg that had stabbed the ground beside me, slowly rises before my face and I flinch back, only to realize, that Gary's keys now hang from its sharp-clawed end, flashing silver in the limited moonlight. He's offering it to me.

"Oh." I cup my hands together, and with a resonant jingle, he drops the damp, cold key ring into my waiting palms.

I crane my neck to peer up at the hole that I'd fallen through. The trees above stand hunched over the opening, releasing their rainwater from their overhanging knobby branches and exposed roots in a steady drip.

A ray of moonlight shows me how far I'd really dropped. Tens and tens of feet, it's a wonder I didn't break anything. It's a wonder I'm still alive.

“I can’t get out of here,” I say softly. My eyes widen in the dark when his silhouetted form bends into a bowed position from high above.

“Then, I’ll take you,” he says gently. I remain rooted to the ground. The broken bones, and cocoons of the dead surrounding me are seared in my mind, and knowing he is the one responsible makes it almost too unbearable to look at him, to be so close. I feel sick.

“I have told you already that I have no interest in eating you. I have no desire of anything from you, but for you to leave...as quickly as possible. If you wish the same, you have no choice but to trust me.” He remains bowed, waiting for my approach.

This was true. If he wanted to devour me, he could've made quick work of me like he had Gary.

Reaching out through the darkness, my hand grazes something long and silky, but not sticky.

*Is this hair?*

I grip onto it, and he lets out something like a muffled hiss. I yank my hands back in apology, "Sorry!" I say, self-consciously.

I tentatively reach out to him again, and I feel him lower himself to my level. My fingers glide across smooth bare skin; it's hot but not scalding, his warmth is somehow reassuring. At my touch, I hear him deepen a breath that he'd been holding.

I feel the gentle rise of a heaving chest, its firm give beneath my fingertips, then the deep ripple of abs... my hands trace his shape, following crisp angles of defined musculature. This close, there is no missing the sheer size of him. Standing before me, he's taller than any man has the right to be, given his long segmented spider-like appendages.

*But on top, he feels human...what the hell?*

Sephtis snatches my hand, halting my investigation.

"Please," I hear him say tightly, "take my hand."

I can tell he's trying not to sound impatient, but it's slightly condescending. I grip his strong, much-too-human hand, I'm hauled from the ground and just about tossed over his shoulder onto his back. And now the differences are made much more clear. His top half is almost identical to that of a man, is that of a man's, but his bottom half is where I really see–and feel it.

It's spider-like in every way, chitinous and hard, with a thorax, a bulbous abdomen, and eight thick, long, spidery legs that held him in the air, just as he was. This part of him is covered in what I can only guess is a smooth exoskeleton, as dark as the deepest shadows. The overall effect is unsettling, but also strangely intriguing in a twisted sort of way.

I feel my own heart quicken as he begins to move, and I clutch him around the waist to keep from losing my balance. His muscles tighten beneath my grip, and he quickens his pace.

"Hold on tightly," His voice is still calm, but now it has an edge. We rise and fall across the uneven ground until he begins at a steep vertical incline and begins to scale the dirt walls of the pit, and I feel my stomach drop. My grip around him tightens, I keep my head down, my face buried in his slick dark hair that flows curtain-like down his back. His scent is earthy and rich, a strange mix of woody and spice I can't quite put my finger on at the moment. It's a pleasantly dizzying aroma.

We're moving exceptionally fast, and the light of the night sky increases, revealing the pale skin of his shoulders, veined with what looks to be thin black markings and of which I realize, there are four. And four arms, one pair set below the other so that there are two upper and two lower. As he scales the wall, he brushes aside the occasional debris, or broken tree limbs snagged on silvery webbing with his hands, or a long clawed foreleg. I try to get a view of his face, but the sharp line of his jaw is all that is visible to me from this angle.

Almost reaching the top of the drop-off, he jerks to a halt. “You will have to go the rest of the way alone,” he says. “I cannot leave here.”

“But, why?” I breathe before I can stop myself.

“That...is none of your concern.” He says, and there's a sharpness to his tone. “Grab the root, and climb up. I’ve taken you as far as I will go.”

Sephtis's movements are quick, as he points to a hanging root above me. Despite his proximity, I still can’t get a clear look at him, and my curiosity burns. Despite it, I release him and grip onto the root above me. The earth loosens slightly, and I wonder if it will hold.

"It will hold." He assures me as though having read my mind.

Anchoring myself, I feel strangely reluctant to leave him— he feels much more sturdy than these flimsy roots. He makes the decision for me when he carefully lowers himself beneath me and leaves me to dangle from the thick hanging tendrils. After a moment of probing, I find a foothold and secure myself there.

I quickly glance down, but it's only to glimpse the head of dark sleek hair sink further from sight, receding back into the deep recesses and shadows of the crevasse below.

I climb up until Sephtis is far in the distance. Pulling myself up, I just manage to shimmy over the edge of the pit and roll onto my back, on damp earth and grass. Finally, I release a massive breath of relief. I can almost hear the quiet slink of him below, then again, he could be long gone already.

I sit up, peering over the ledge into the vast darkness below, and call out to him all the same:

"I’m sorry you can’t leave!" I say, "No one should have to be alone.”

No answer comes back, there is only the deathly silence of the abyss.

I pause and bite the side of my lip. "And thank you for, in your own way, saving me..."

Again, nothing.

I'm sore, soaked, dirtied, and drenched, but far too grateful to be alive to care. I sigh, gingerly managing to pull myself to my feet and look around.

The rain has stopped. It's hard to tell in the dark, but it looks like the earth has been churned over around the area where I'd fallen. There are indentations and cracks, and a few trees have toppled over.

I take off into the night, back in the direction I'd come from. High beams stretch through the woods before me, the light is a beacon in the dark, a welcome sight, and my heart lifts in my chest when I realize I've made it.

The car's doors are still hanging open. I walk around to the passenger's side and push the door closed, then sling myself into the driver's seat, throwing Gary's things onto the floor, and turn the key. The engine sputters but comes to life.

The dashboard clock reads after 10PM. Wrapping my hands around the wheel, I look towards the woods again, then shake my head. I pull out onto the main road, throw the car into drive, and accelerate.

But what– rather who I found in the pit, Sephtis, is what I can't stop thinking about. Definitely not a man, but not quite a beast.

# Rhianne

Reaching the comforting familiarity of my cul-de-sac, I pull the car into the driveway of my home but wait a while in the parked vehicle, turning the lights out and sitting in the dark for a long time trying to process what just happened. When that doesn't work, I finally pull my aching body out of Gary's car, and reaching my front porch, unlock my door and go in, locking the door behind myself. All time seems to stand still. Shakingly, I run my hands over my blood and rain-soaked clothes.

Memories of my assault resurface, the crazed look in Gary's eyes as he grabbed, then struck me. I felt so helpless then, and now rage rises up from deep within, anger that I couldn't do anything to stop him. But then, these are juxtaposed by Gary's screams. They ring clear in my ears, the snapping of his bones, the cocoons strewn along the pit, the horror of the night.

Sinking to the floor and hugging myself, for the first time that night, I sob. Hot tears sting my eyes, then pour down my cheeks. My trembling lips part, and I whisper the name that has become a permanent fixture in my memories. "Sephtis..."

The utterance of his name alone makes the air seem to stir around me. The walls and floors of my home seem to vibrate. Goose flesh rises along my limbs, and a chill runs down my spine. Without warning, a loud crackle erupts before me, and I recoil.

A guttural shrill erupts from my throat when a massive unmoving figure appears sprawled out directly across from me.

Staring at it, I wait for movement, but...nothing. I rise to unsteady feet and take a step, then another, my eyes saucered. When I am within touching distance, I finally recognize what I'm looking at.

Black lacing with a diamond shine creates unique patterns on rain-slick ashen flesh and stops just at the base of a pale throat. Long dark hair obscures his face and cascades over his shoulders to his lower back. Queerer still, I can clearly see his not one pair of arms, but two.

As he pulls himself more upright, I see his breathing is shallow, and his toned, muscular chest leads to a trim waist of an otherwise human-like torso, but what intrigues and terrifies me the most is the disturbing deviance of his lower half now completely visible in the light. Behind what appears to be a silken loin cloth over Sephtis's hips, is a smooth black spiderlike thorax and abdomen and four pairs of segmented legs protruding from them. Smooth and hard all at once, glistening as though shined with polish.

*It's him. Somehow, he's here.*

Standing before him, I let my trembling fingers push his hair from his face and very nearly gasp. Handsome would be an understatement; he is ethereal, almost surreal– facially at least. My breath catches, my eyes taking in every detail, his sculpted jawline, his high cheekbones.

With lightning swiftness, Sephtis captures my wrist in a hand, and I freeze, my heart thundering in my chest. Placing my palm flat to his cheek, he opens his eyes, and I gaze into a red so deep that they appear like cut rubies, surrounded by dark shining sclerae and a fringe of equally dark lashes.

Tentative, I trace my thumb over his full, sensual lips. As if in a trance, he parts them slightly, letting out a hiss-like groan before slowly wrapping an enormous black foreleg around my waist, shepherding me into his radius in a way that is half-longing and half-gentle.

“Well, this is a turn of events,” he says hazily.

“I don’t understand. I-Is this a dream? Wha-How...Why are you here?” I stammer.

Only a soft chuckle escapes his lips, as though he too is incredulous. "I could ask you the same thing." Then he gives me a small smile, revealing a glint of needle-sharp, inch-long fangs. “You brought me here, Amata.”

“I told you, my name is Rhianne, and no– I don’t think I did.”

I try to retract my hand, but he curls his fingers gently around mine and runs his soft lips lightly across the knuckles of my hand. I can't help the ripple of electricity, and the shiver that comes and goes through me.

“You called out to me. And I know your name. I addressed you as *Amata* for a reason.”

I scarcely dare to breathe, “And why's that?”

He lifts a hand to caress the side of my face, making warmth crawl up my neck and cheeks. “Because where I’m from, Amata is a term of affection we give to our destined wives.”

# Sephtis

I let my fingers trail down her jaw and gauge her reaction. Her soft skin is creamy smooth, both warm and supple; as with all humans, she looks to me so frail.

I watch her eyes move down my body and back up again. The woman called Rhianne pulls away from me and stumbles backward, but I keep a leg around her waist to steady her before she can fall. If I had such an unstable build as she, I'd likely need steadying too. It's no wonder she needed protecting, such an impractical and delicate frame.

The slow drop of her brow reveals her confusion. "What did you just say?"

"You heard me," I say as I move to kneel in a more comfortable position. The chamber is not very high; pulling myself up to my full standing height would be a bit uncomfortable. I contemplate the best way to put this, but decide the best way to do it is just to be straight-forward. "I'm here because...you're my wife."

Rhianne's eyes dilate, and she looks me over again, I can feel her heart pounding beneath her soft human flesh, and can't help but relish the feeling.

"That doesn't make sense." She presses a hand to her breast, and I find my gaze lingering there. "I don't know what you're talking about, and I don't know how you got here, but it's your turn to leave."

I can tell she's uncomfortable and afraid— but I also sense her fascination. I step closer to her trying to keep my movements slow and easy, only the sound of my claws clicking against the unnaturally smooth surface of the polished floors fills the air between us.

She's so small, I quite easily dwarf her, and I watch a storm of emotions wash over her face. I can see the movement of her breaths, her chest rising with each intake of air. Her scent fills the air around her, a hint of sweet jasmine and vanilla, with just a touch of the most subtle feminine musk— her own natural scent. I could almost taste her, an intoxicating mixture of these.

It's hard not to want to savor that fragrance— the same one that lured me back in my lair. She's so close, I can feel the heat radiating off of her body. I want to reach out to her, to take her in my arms and hold her. I want to make her mine; another part of me craves more...

Her heart rate has definitely increased, but there's no indication of outright panic, at least not yet. Rhianne trembles before me, struggling to keep herself calm, rational, and aware, she whispers: "This is impossible. I-it's impossible."

I nod once, and I very nearly chuckle. "Yes, I would agree. But still, it's true."

This is just as unexpected for myself. When I'd helped her leave, it had been with the expectation that I would never see her again– even if part of me yearned to. Yet here I am, standing in front of the woman who unknowingly had control over me.

I'd thought I'd be torn, my mind boggled by this new development; here before me stands the woman who has the ability to summon me to her, to control me. As I continue to look at my wife, I catch myself thinking:

*I'm...not against this.*

Shapely would be an understated term to describe the roadmap of curves that was her frame. Her espresso skin reminds me of a forbidden chocolate I'd heard of, but thought was only a myth. Sticks and leaves are ensnared in her full, long, raven hair, leaving it in a mess of coils and curls tangled on top of her head. It doesn't matter. If anything, it helps and allows me to look into the deepest brown eyes I've ever seen. Her eyelashes fan out like butterfly wings, sitting subtly on top of her soft doe-like eyes.

My lips part slightly, as I stare into her eyes, my breathing heavy, in this moment, it's as though she has me caught, as helpless as any creature entangled tightly in a web.

Just like that, I am hers.

"Sephtis— "

I can see a hint of deep-set dimples in her cheeks every time she parts her full lips to say something that I'm far too distracted to hear. She is gorgeous, and the more I look at how flustered she is, the more the idea of being tied to her proves quite appealing.

"Are you even listening to me?!" she shouts, pulling me from my thoughts. Even her shout sounds musical to me. Her arms are held tightly across her chest, her cheeks flushed.

She rubs her forehead and mutters, "Great. Human or not, men still don't listen."

Only then do I manage to snap out of my trance. "It's not that I wasn't listening, it's just that I know nothing you say will change things." I say, trying hard to continue looking into her eyes rather than at her form. "Only our wives can command us. You called out to me, and here I am. If I weren't tied to you, that wouldn't have happened. It's fated, Amata..."

I hear her growl in frustration.

"Did you just growl at me?" My eyes narrow on her, and she glares right back. I mildly admire her unexpected fierceness; in the pit, she'd been so much more timid. I feel suddenly that I want to experience the many facets of her, to know every side of her, everything about her—

"Yes! Because you're not listening to me, and now you're being a smartass!" She paused. "Wait. Why don't you sound all archaic *Riddler* like you did earlier?"

I squint again, unfamiliar with her apparent reference, and she stifles a laugh. "Just asking."

This is the first moment I've seen her smile, and I decide she looks quite beautiful when she does.

"I'm guessing you're not a comic book person?" She says.

I shake my head. "No, I am not. But, my people can acclimate to new cultures and climates quickly. Within a few days, I'll blend right in. So, you have nothing to worry about."

She simply stares at me in disbelief for a long several moments, before finally, she whispers to herself: "This is not real; you're not real." She glares at me again. "None of this...it can't be. I hit my head earlier. I'm seeing things."

She's gone back into denial again. Even if I want her to feel comfortable in front of me, to feel at ease, I can't resist giving her a small taste of just how real this is.

Fluidly extending my legs, I completely close the gap between us. I feel her body tense as I lower my head, extend my tongue and run the tip of it up the side of her neck, along her jaw, up her cheek. I feel her temperature rise several degrees beneath my tongue, though she trembles like she's cold. She's velvety smooth and so soft, her flavor is entirely addictive...

I hear her gasp and revel in the way her chest rises with the hitching of her breath.

"This is real, I am real." I breathe, my voice comes out thickly. I pause, looking into her eyes. She looks a little dazed.

"We can work," I assure her. "I'm not that different from you. If you need time to adjust, I can give you time. Soon enough, we will do anything normal married couples of your species do."

# Rhianne

I can't help but gawk at him in all of his abnormalcy. His deep red eyes shine, and despite the inherent beauty of his features, they are carved with a chiseled intensity that suggests a vicious ferocity, like those ancient warriors whose skill with the blade was matched only by a thirst for blood. His body, the human-looking part of it anyway, is the epitome of masculinity, but that's where his similarities to a man start and end. Tonight he proved he's more terrifying than any man, and I'm not sure I'm comfortable calling him one.

After what I saw of him in that pit, I'm not sure I want to be near him. He is too fast, too strong— the memory of it makes me pause and shudder, makes me want to run away from what I know is standing before me. Danger in the form of an eight-foot-tall man-spider, and taller still if he chose to stand at full height. Even if I did make a run for it, I likely wouldn't make it three steps before he caught me.

"Normal?" I repeat him, incredulous.

He quirks his head in question, causing his long black curtain of hair to spill over one shoulder. He crosses his lower set of arms and strokes his chin thoughtfully with an upper one.

“Normal-ish." he corrects himself, then ponders to himself. "What exactly would those things be?...Never mind, we have a lifetime to figure it out.”

“God, will you stop!” I exclaim, throwing my arms up. I step back and out of the circle of his grasp. I've reached the limit of my patience. “Listen to me. We are NOT married. I don’t know what your home rules are, but here, at the bare minimum, you and your spouse should be anatomically matched. And I’m sorry if that’s offensive, I’m just saying I doubt it would go over well if I brought a half-man half-spider to the company party.” I say, gesturing emphatically at his entirety.

But, reality hits me like a freight train as the words leave my mouth. I'd have to be at work tomorrow. I feel the blood drain from my face as Gary flashes in my mind. I glance down at the scattered droplets of blood marring my blouse and skirt.

“Shit! Why did I drive Gary’s car here?!” I place my head in my hands and squeeze my eyes shut. “Everything’s going to point to me when he doesn’t show up. Shit, I’m going to lose my job. I’m going to go to jail...they'd never believe me if I told them the truth— I’m covered in his blood!— ”

My chest feels like it’s caving in on itself, my breath feels shallow, and I’m so dizzy that I fear I might faint. I feel hot, feverish even, my heart is racing and pounding in my chest. I can’t even catch my breath, can’t seem to get enough air, and I'm desperate for it.

Electricity shoots through me as firm hands land heavily on my shoulders.

“Don’t panic. Everything will be fine,” The deep timbre of Sephtis's voice is somehow comforting, I can feel the heat of his palms through my shirt. But I fight it.

I begin to laugh mirthlessly, he's the one who caused this in the first place. Well, I suppose not entirely...Gary did have it coming, the bastard.

But, still, "That's easy for you to s—"

Opening my eyes, my jaw goes slack, and I nearly fall again at the sight of the gloriously nude man before me.

He's more compact now, but still substantial, standing nearly head and shoulders above me. Without his spidery legs, standing at full height would no longer have him threatening to breach the ceiling—and speaking of shoulders, I notice he's down to only two arms.

He has a little more color in his skin now, a healthy glow. And as my eyes traverse the rippling lines of his muscular torso, they widen when they reach the phallus between his thickly muscled thighs. It is positively massive, thick, semi-hard, and hanging low between his legs. It seems that what little he had to wear slipped off of him during the transformation. It only makes the breathlessness in my chest worse. I meet his gaze again, and I'm met with much more toned down, deep mahogany-hued irises and perfectly human sclerae— though his eyes are just as hypnotic as before.

Amused by my reaction, he slowly tilts his head to the side, and a small smile plays at the corner of his lips. "Now I know of at least one thing that will ease your panic," he speaks, his tone teasing. "This is my human form. I take it from the look on your face, you agree we are *at the bare minimum, anatomically matched*?"

"You would destroy me," I blurt, then quickly slam my hand over my mouth, heat rising up my face.

"Adorable." He chuckles softly, sending a ripple of goosebumps across my skin. "And, what if I promise to be gentle?"

He runs his fingertips down my shoulders in a feather-light caress and of its own volition, my whole body shudders pleasurably from the sensation. I can't believe he's making me feel this way. I need to get away from him. Now.

I push away from his touch and nearly sprint from the room. "I'm taking a shower!" I toss over a shoulder, before bolting up the winding staircase as I make for the bathroom.

I lock the bathroom door and lean against it, pressing my palm against my chest. My heart is still racing a mile a minute, but this time, it's for a whole different reason.

I struggle to peel my saturated clothing off of my body. Fumbling with the control panel of the shower, I try my best to cleanse the sinful thoughts from my mind.

I stand under the showerhead for nearly twenty minutes, letting the water rush over my body, trying to wash away the memory of Gary, of Sephtis, of everything earlier tonight. I scrub myself raw, it doesn't help. Nothing can. I lean against the shower tiles and give in.

It's difficult to deny that Sephtis is a very attractive man. But the fact remains, he's not human. He may have saved me once, but he's something dangerous, and now he's in my house.

I close my eyes. But behind my eyelids, I only picture Sephtis behind me, pressing himself against me. With a tremulous gasp, a ripple of pleasure runs through my body at the thought of it. His hands on my body, on my face, his lips against mine. I imagine his thick, manhood thrusting inside of me, his cock filling me so completely I can't help but cry out.

But then I let out a cry of frustration. What am I thinking? I can't possibly want this. The wild, inexplicable attraction I feel towards him must simply be my mind's way of dealing with the trauma of this evening, nothing more.

*That's it, Rhianne, you're just reacting to the stress of the situation.*

However, something deep inside me doesn't fully accept my reasoning.

# Sephtis

I watch, dumbstruck at the steps Rhianne has retreated up, I can see that I've made her uncomfortable, to say the least. Normally, I'd be fine with that— I'm used to humans being much less than calm in my presence. But this time, I'm not. I've just taken on a new role, one I must equip myself for.

I know how to be a hunter, a predator, even a monster...but, at the moment I am uncertain how to proceed as I refasten the cloth about my waist. She has made it clear that she needs me to let her set the pace, that I need to follow her lead. It's been many years since I've had to deign to negotiate with anyone, or to submit myself to the wants of another...it's not something that comes naturally to me.

This is going to be difficult, I realize. I stare after her departure a moment longer, then shake my head. I know she would be opposed should I follow her to her shower.

I frown at the thought of her naked body, concealed by a flimsy door, and can't help imagining what she must look like soaking in the water.

I see it as plain as day, my mind bringing it into focus, the water glistening on her slick deep brown skin, soaking her dark, beautiful coiling hair, running down her backside and legs, coating her like a second skin, her breasts rising and falling with each breath. I can imagine her hands, sliding up her body, caressing, exploring. And suddenly, in my mind's eye, her hands are on me, my chest, my stomach, stroking me.

I get a swift, unexpected picture of her on her knees, the shaft of my cock sliding between her full, plump lips, I can see it so clearly. Her darting those dark eyes up at me as she takes me deeper. The thought is too much to bear.

But that very thought is interrupted by a faint, and muffled cry issuing from her bathroom— it's quiet, mostly drowned out by the sound of rushing water, but my hearing is inhumanly acute. I stiffen, shocked, it's a cry I've heard before, one that I know comes from pleasure. But the next one is different. Her second cry is filled with a desperation that leaves me cold, it ripples through my whole being. It sounds as if she's distressed.

It's difficult to resist the urge to run to her, and see what is wrong. Is she in pain? Someone couldn't have broken in, I'd have heard them... and though I do sense an additional presence in the house, it's nothing that rouses any concern in me.

I pause, uncertain. Rhianne didn't want me to follow, but I don't like the sound of her shout.

With a sudden burst of speed, I race upstairs. I need to ensure she's okay, even if it means she'll be upset with me. Pausing at the chamber door, I listen, trying to separate one echo from another; I hear the water running, and her breathing.

I frown, confused. "Rhianne, are you alright? Open this door!"

# Rhianne

I startle hearing Sephtis's deep, resonant voice issue from right outside the bathroom door. I try to quiet myself, but I'm unsure if I'm successful.

The concern in his voice sounds genuine: "I heard you cry out. You sounded upset. Answer me, Rhianne!"

My face flushes, I feel warmth flowing into my cheeks again. I wonder just how much he'd heard, and how long he'd been there. My fingers fumble with the shower panel, turning the water off.

"I'm fine," I call back finally, then my voice softens. "I'm just a little shaken up, that's all. Nothing to worry about, I'm just...finishing up."

I step out of the shower, drying hastily and pulling a thick, fluffy towel around my body. I hear a brief pause on the other side of the door. "I understand this is difficult for you, but I will never hurt you, I swear it. I know I've said that before, but I need you to believe me."

"I know," I reply, though I'm uncertain if I actually do. Taking a final breath, I open the door a crack, releasing tendrils of steam out into the hall. I peek through, my eyes meeting his from beneath my lashes. He studies me intently, perhaps trying to decide how much I'm withholding from him.

"I'm feeling a lot better now," I add quickly, opening the door further. He steps forward, and instinctively, I step back.

“Rhianne— ” The crease in his brow deepens. He knows better.

"Really," I insist.

I can tell it's difficult for him to let it go, but eventually, he drops it.

"...I'll take your word for it." The sigh in his voice fades, held out momentarily in the air between us. But his expression is still unreadable as he looks at me, his smoldering eyes scanning the expanse of my form. He drifts his gaze over me in obvious appreciation of the towel I'm wrapped in. My heart skips a beat as I watch him drink me in.

"Um, you can use the shower now," I say quickly, motioning to the bathroom behind me, and sidestepping him before he can utter another word. Brushing passed him sends an inexplicable rippling of heat up my arm.

"Wait—" His voice is low, husky, and soft.

I find myself halting mid-step, I cast a glance over a shoulder back at him to find him exactly where I left him.

"What?" I ask warily.

He turns to look at me, shifting his weight, his eyes never leaving mine. He says a bit sheepishly. "I've only ever bathed in rivers and lakes. Anything else has been a bit old-fashioned...I've never used a bath like this before." For a moment, his gaze flickers from mine, before he meets my eyes once more from the distance of several steps across the hall. "Will you show me how it works?"

I watch him, startled by the admission. I study his face, hard, certain that it's a lie. But instead of the gleam of a trickster, I find he's completely serious as he stands there, and as I look at him, I can see a faint flush spreading up his neck, over his cheekbones, and across his strong jawline.

I can't help but find this aspect of him quite human, almost endearing, his embarrassment on the matter quite evident. He runs a hand through his hair. "Nevermind, I'll figure it out..." His voice trails off, and I realize he's trying to be considerate of me.

"No..." I say, despite myself, it's suddenly difficult to resist the urge to smile, and softening, I find myself taking an unexpected step towards him.

"You better stand back," I warn him, uncertainty in my voice.

He steps out of the way, and lets me pass.

"It's easy enough," I say, wanting to get this over with as quickly as possible. "A shower like this," I point to the chrome shower head, "delivers water through a hose-like apparatus. You turn it on here." I point to the control panel on the wall.

Then I demonstrate turning on the water. It comes out of the shower head at the proper position, and I adjust it to a warmer setting. He watches me intently, his deep mahogany eyes trained on my every move, and I feel my flesh warm under that gaze.

"It's pretty self-explanatory after that. There are a few options for temperature, pressure, things like that."

I'm surprised by the consistent warmth in my cheeks, unsure if it's due to my embarrassment or the fact that he watches me so closely. Our eyes lock, I can almost see the red heat in his eyes.

"I have shampoo you can use too...you're, um, good to go."

He steps out of what little clothes he's already wearing, and it's hard to ignore the utter perfection of his form. I move back, allowing him room to step into the tub. He steps into the stream, and I watch the warm water trickle down the taut lines of his chest and the deep ridges of his abs. As water pours down on him, it slicks his long midnight hair down to his flesh.

"And those?" Sephtis says, pointing at the shower gel and loofah sitting in the caddy.

"Those? Oh, okay, sure. It's like this..."

Picking up both, I lather up the loofah. I consider it for a moment, and my gaze drifts back to his body. He stands in a relaxed posture, he's so comfortable in his nakedness, standing before me, fully on display. I take in the pure masculinity of his form, his strength, and power roll off of him in waves. Suddenly, I feel a deep longing in my core to explore it...

I know I can just hand him the loofah, instead, something in me compels me. I reach out and press it against Sephtis's torso, and watch his abs clench as I do, his skin blossoming in goose flesh. I draw the bath sponge across his chest, and I watch the playful trail of bubbles follow the path of the loofah. I find my fingers now tracing the intricate patterns of deeply etched black lines that decorate his skin like lace, a net tattooed over the expanse of his flesh. It's beautiful...

He tilts his head back, and his breathing labors with each stroke of my wrist as I bathe him, and I see his gaze linger on my face, travel down my body, settling for a moment at the swell of my breasts then resting on the towel wrapped around me. He places his hand on top of mine, stilling it, and the current of desire that courses through me surprises me.

I glance up at him, and have my gaze returned by glowing red eyes filled with desire. I squeeze my knees together tightly, hoping that it might diminish the sensation which flows through me. It's foreign and intense, unlike anything I've ever felt, and I know I should back away. But I don't, I can't. Gently, he lifts his other hand to my face, cradling it softly in his palm.

Startled, I pull back and drop the sponge, breaking the spell and immediately follow with a murmured apology. "Sorry...I..."

I start to turn away, embarrassed once more by my clumsiness, but he places his hand on my arm, stilling me.

“Don’t apologize for touching what belongs to you,” His voice comes huskily.

I look up at him, and I’m stunned at the sincere reverence in his expression. He’s looking at me like I’m something precious, and he takes his time, his eyes memorizing every feature of my face.

“I-I’ll leave a towel and spare toothbrush out, my brother left some of his clothes in the guest room on his last visit a while back. You can stay the night, and we’ll figure something out in the morning,” I say, and he nods once.

"Goodnight, Rhianne," he replies in a low rumble, and I can hear the longing behind his words, slowly, he turns back to the shower's warm gentle rain, closing his eyes, his expression relaxing and softening at the sensation of the warm water.

I scurry back out into the hall, making my way to my bedroom, and close the door behind. Then, letting out a shuddering breath, I lean against the door for support. My heart is pounding, my blood swimming with a heady, bittersweet mix of adrenaline, raw chemistry, and a strange melancholy, a longing for the impossible.

I scan my room until I locate my pajamas and walk over to dress for bed. From any perspective, I know how incredibly strange this situation is. A "man-spider"—a "spider-man"? is sleeping under my roof for the night, a man who is both dangerous and oddly attractive.

Despite my internal warning system blasting danger, an unmistakable desire is stirring inside of me, dangerously close to the surface. I flump back onto the cool cotton-softness of my mattress, just as a ball of orange fluff jumps up onto my comforter. Drawing my legs up off the floor to sit cross-legged, I take the warm ball of fur up into my arms.

"Hey, Mr. Muffins," I smile, "There you are."

I only just realize I haven't seen my cat all night. I wonder if he'd hidden seeing that I had a new house guest.

"Mr. Muffins, you're a coward."

Mr. Muffins merely stretches out in my lap for a belly rub, and I stroke him absent-mindedly, his purring putting me at ease. Things almost feel normal. I finally set Mr. Muffins aside and resolve to get some sleep.

With a deep breath, I close my eyes. Tomorrow will come soon enough, and with it, another day of dealing with this bizarre situation, but for now at least, sleep beckons me into its warm embrace.

# Rhianne

*What the hell is wrong with me?*

I chastise myself as I toss and turn for the hundredth time. Sephtis had long said goodnight, and made his way to the guest bedroom, but I can't stop thinking about him. Within hours, he's gone from something that terrifies me to someone who puts thoughts in my mind that I know I shouldn't be having.

*Well, technically, I can have them since he is my husband.* I rub my forehead. *Really, Rhianne?*

I know I should be more freaked out than I am. There are still so many questions to be answered, but after the events of tonight, I can't dredge up the energy to ask. I clench my thighs together, but the tingle remains.

*Stop being such a hornball. He's not even human.*

Even though my eyelids are heavy and tired, bound by exhaustion, I can't sleep. I can't get the image of him out of my mind, his voice out of my head. I can almost hear it now:

"Please..."

*Please?*

At the sound of the muffled voice, I bolt up in bed and strain my ears to listen.

"Please...no," Sephtis's voice, breathy and thick with emotion, issues through the wall from the guest room, and I freeze. His voice sounds desperate, pleading. “Don't make me—” He rasps.

Something is wrong.

I toss the covers off of myself and slip out of my bed.

Walking across the hall to the door to Sephtis's room, I soon stop, hesitating. I barely know him, and yet, I feel compelled to do something to help him.

Taking a deep breath, I push open the door. My heart thuds as I walk closer to inspect. The room is mostly dark, but the first hint of dawn is coming through the windows, painting Sephtis's form with purple light. I can see he's curled up in a ball on the bed, fully clothed, and shaking. His arms are wrapped tightly around himself, his breath coming in heavy gasps. His face is drawn, his eyes squeezed closed as though he were in pain.

“Please...no...I'm sorry—don't leave me...” His voice is strained, it sounds like he is pleading with himself as well as someone else. The sorrow in it pierces my heart like a knife.

Fear floods over me. What do I do? What do I say? How can I help him?

Reaching out towards him, I bite my lip in hesitation, then I place a tentative hand on his shoulder. “Sephtis,” I say, gently shaking him. “Sephtis, wake up—”

His head snaps up, and he jolts upright, his eyes glowing red, feral. He growls but instead of attacking me, he glances around the room, confused, before his eyes find mine.

“Rhianne?"

“I'm here,” I say, offering him a small reassuring smile.

"W-what happened?" He asks, alertness returning instantly to him. "Are you okay?"

"Me? I...well, yes—"

Before I can react, Sephtis pulls me against himself into an embrace. His arms are tight around me, and I feel his chest heave with the force required for him to take in great shuddering gulps of air. "Thank goodness," He says, breathless. "Thank goodness—"

The shock of his sudden action leaves me breathless. My hands come up automatically, one gently stroking the back of his head and the other resting on his shoulder. I'm surprised at myself when I don't immediately pull away, nor feel the fear that I had from earlier today. I can smell the natural scent of his skin, something like earthy sandalwood, and Oudh and I feel warmth emanating off of him and into me. It hits me that I don't *want* to pull away. The fear and confusion of the night make way for a feeling so natural, comforting even.

"But, you were the one crying out in your sleep," I reply in a murmur.

Pulling back, Sephtis's eyes widen, then narrow, a question in his gaze.

"You were dreaming. Hearing you worried me...it sounded like you were having a really unpleasant nightmare."

His body stiffens, and he exhales deeply and then turns away from me, running a hand through thick black locks. "I'm sorry for waking you. I don't know what came over me. It won't happen again," he murmurs, drawing away and increasing the space between us.

"Are you sure?"

"Yes, don't worry about me." He says before he schools his features back into stern neutrality. "You should really get some rest, Rhianne. You've been through a lot tonight...I've already put you through a lot of trouble."

"It's really okay— the way I see it, I owed you one anyway." I shrug. "I want to make sure you're alright." I'm not usually this person. I'm not usually someone who goes around comforting people yet somehow I'm doing it now? Aside from feeling like a burden, I can tell he wants his space, and I retract my hand, and rise to my feet.

"Rhianne, before you go, I need you to answer a question honestly," He speaks, avoiding my gaze. "The bruising on your face, was that from your fall or from the man I killed?"

This is the first time he'd mentioned Gary, or what had happened tonight in those woods.

I'm almost reluctant to admit what happened earlier tonight, I raise a hand to the sore, tight spot on my cheek, my fingertips grazing my skin gingerly. "It wasn't the fall," I say finally, and see him grit his teeth in response, I see his fangs lengthen further in his mouth, and it startles me.

"I will take care of everything in the morning. You have nothing to worry about," he says to me over his shoulder, I nod in response. I don't think he quite realizes the type of predicament I'm in, that he truly can't do anything to help me; the sentiment is appreciated though. "Goodnight." He says.

I sigh. "...I hope you have better dreams, Sephtis."

"You're kind, Rhianne. Thank you."

"Of course."

As I cross the room, I hear him softly utter, "I'll never let anyone hurt you again. That is my word."

# Rhianne

Sephtis presses the flats of his palms into my thighs, spreading me. He takes his time, bringing his mouth to my inner thigh, trailing scorching kisses along my flesh that make me shiver in anticipation. Parting his lips, he runs his tongue closer and closer to where I need him to be. I arch my back, while he continues his torturous exploration, lightly scratching the inside of my thigh with his teeth.

Sephtis's gaze finds mine, and he smiles, flashing a hint of fang. I feel the heat of his eyes; he is enjoying this, seeing me lose control, he is almost merciless as he tastes me.

"I've waited far too long for this," he says, his breath warm against my center, it sends delicious shocks up my spine.

"I have too, so please, Sephtis—"

My plea is interrupted by a flick of Sephtis's tongue against my weeping sex, heating me up almost instantly. I moan and shift my hips, when he finds my pleasure spot quickly, and I hold onto the smooth wood of the headboard for dear life.

I cry out, shuddering as he massages the slick folds of my flesh with his tongue. His hands slip beneath me, palming my ass, before gripping my flesh roughly and yanking me closer to him.

I realize how much I love his coarse, gifted tongue against my soft skin, his warm, wet mouth on my dripping wetness. The feeling of his fangs against my sensitive, swollen clit has me quivering and begging for release.

"Fuck, please Sephtis, don't stop!" I moan. "Please...I can't take it anymore."

He smiles against my skin, holds me steady, and drives his tongue deep into my center.

*Beep, Beep, Beep*

The shrill cry of the alarm tears me from my dream, and I nearly jump upright in my bed. Reaching between my legs, I groan at the feeling of my damp panties.

I'm exhausted. The remainder of my night had consisted of growing concern over Sephtis's nightmare and heated dreams of all the things he could do to me.

I slam my hand into my comforter. *What is happening to me?*

Pulling myself from my bed, I wrap my robe around my body. It's still early, and if I'm lucky, I can probably escape the house and avoid talking to Sephtis until I have time to clear my head.

I hurry with my morning routine, and dress for work. I've managed to mostly cover the mark left by Gary yesterday, but I still feel sore all over.

Rubbing the back of my neck, I attempt to stretch the stiffness away, but the sound of a deep yowl, and a clatter brings me to pause. I listen closely against the door, and the yowl grows from low to full-out panic.

*What the hell?--*

I yank the door open, and race down the stairs.

Sprinting to the kitchen, I stop in my tracks and stare as the intimidating Sephtis sits, scrunched on the counter, brandishing a spatula like a sword at something on the floor I can't quite make out.

Unsure of what I'm witnessing, I draw closer, and my eyes widen at something writhing on the floor tiles. Tufts of orange fur peek out from the silk webbing surrounding it. My cat is still yowling, and I can hear him panting. I don't know what to do.

"Get it away from me!" Sephtis exclaims, his eyes wide and fangs bared in a snarl as he flaps the spatula back and forth.

"What the hell Sephtis?! Why did you web Mr. Muffins?!" I shriek, scrambling to my knees beside the helpless, yowling cat, entangled by webbing.

"What is a *Mr. Muffins*?" Sephtis flinches back and darts me a look.

"Mr. Muffins is my cat! Why the heck did you web my cat?!"

Sephtis's lips curve downwards into a frown. "I didn't mean to, it landed on my web as I was trying to catch you breakfast! I tried to free the hell cat, and then it struck out and scratched me!" He pouts at me and shows me the scratch on his pinky. "It hurt, too. Mr. Muffins might sound delicious in theory, but I assure you, he is NOTHING of the sort."

I look from the small helpless cat, to Sephtis's frame as he tries to maintain his station on the counter. I'm not sure if I should laugh or be offended. Unable to hold back any longer, I belt out a laugh. I double over and damn-near cackle.

"It's not funny," Sephtis grumbles with a grimace, making me laugh even harder.

I wipe the tears from my eyes. "Okay, okay, I'm done."

Bending over Mr. Muffins, I reach out to untangle him, but Sephtis lunges from the counter. With a speed faster than I can perceive, he grabs my hands before I can begin, and runs his thumbs gently over my knuckles.

"Be careful. You'll get stuck too." He says softly, the warmth of his breath fans across the shell of my ear, sending goosebumps down my arms. I shiver. "I don't want you to get caught."

Sephtis turns me around to face him, and I'm caught by the intensity of his gaze, my hands still in his.

"Okay," I whisper, caught up in the moment.

He chuckles lightly, looking chagrined. "This is not the way I envisioned this going. I must have looked like a complete fool."

"You did...but it was also kind of cute."

"Cute?" He asks, surprised. His eyebrows arch up to his hairline. "Cute. Of all the things you could say about me, you find me 'cute?'"

"What exactly did you expect me to say?" I ask.

He smiles, and it nearly takes my breath away. I clear my throat and stand up straight. "But, for future reference though, a simple avocado toast would suffice--plus, I'm a vegetarian, and in my experience, fruits and veggies don't have a habit of getting up and running away. Here, I have something that should help with your scratch," I feel his gaze hot on me while I move to pull open a nearby kitchen drawer.

He joins me there, and turning to him, I wrap a Band-Aid around his pinky finger and plant a kiss on it. "There, all better. I have some lollipops if you want one to go with your band-aid," I tease.

His eyes go dark, searching mine. "Hilarious. No thanks, but I will take another kiss though..." He says, his voice like silk.

I look up into his eyes. Butterflies flutter in my stomach. "Another kiss?"

"Yes, but this time, how about here..." he breathes, pointing to his lips. "I brushed my teeth, see?" He gives me a grin that leaves me a puddle in my shoes—rather socks. Running his tongue over his fangs, he drawls lustfully. "Minty fresh."

I'm torn between laughter and being unable to breathe.

*How can I argue with that?*

"Fine. One kiss. Better make it count."

"Challenge accepted," he replies.

Sephtis leans over me, bracing one hand on the counter behind me. He rests his other hand lightly on my neck, and my pulse jumps in anticipation. He brings me close, tangling his fingers in my hair.

Slowly, he lowers his lips, and places a featherlight kiss on my cheek. My eyes flutter closed, and I can't help but let out a frustrated whimper.

"What? That didn't count," I say, a little breathless and entirely frustrated.

"Oh? And, what do you want me to do?" He asks, running his thumb in slow circles around my pulse point.

I swallow as he holds me captive in the dark depths of his eyes that make my heart thunder all over again. "You know what I mean—kiss me properly..." I nearly gasp. My fingers thread through his hair, the silky strands sliding their way through my fingers.

This time, he dives in and slants his mouth over mine. His lips are warm and full, and his kiss is deep and tender. I press my hands against his chest. A jolt of awareness travels from our lips down my body.

A low growl rumbles in his chest, and he tightens his fingers in my hair. He gives my bottom lip a small tug with his teeth, and I whimper as I open my mouth, he groans into me, his tongue sweeping inside and tangling with mine. His velvet tongue glides against mine in a sensual dance, and I melt into the kiss. My nipples bead against the inside of my blouse, and a molten ache pools between my thighs; he cups my ass and presses a knee between my legs.

The hair on the back of my neck stands up, and a shiver runs through me. My hands slide over his hard chest, I'm drowning in his kiss, drowning in his arms. I can't seem to get enough of him.

I can feel the hard length of his erection pressing against my lower belly and kiss him harder, losing myself in the intoxicating sensation of his embrace.

All too soon, he pulls away from me, and it feels like he's taken my breath with him.

"I have been waiting to do that since we first met. I thought you were beautiful the moment I laid my eyes on you, Rhianne." His eyes burn into mine as he turns his hand over, slowly tracing a finger down my cheek.

"Well," I say, licking my lips and trying to keep from panting, "I, on the other hand, don't believe I can call you 'cute' at all anymore."

"Oh?" He says, with an arch of a brow. "So then, what do you think I am?"

I take a deep breath and look this dangerous, and handsome man in the eyes. "Sexy."

"Well then..." His eyes darken, and I have to force myself not to squirm. "I'm glad we are of the same opinion."

But soon, he frowns, "I wanted to tell you, you don't need to go to work, Amata."

"I have to—it'd look strange if I didn't. I think." I straighten my clothes. I hear another one of Mr. Muffin's traumatized yowls from beneath the silk netting, drawing our joint attention back to my pet. "Plus, I have to keep the lights on somehow. And, in the meantime, please let Mr. Muffins free."

I disentangle myself from Sephtis's hold.

"I will, I promise, but you promise me you'll grab something to eat on your way to your office," he says, drawing me back to himself and planting a final kiss on my forehead. "Have a good day at work."

It leaves me dizzy, and I damn-near sway on my feet.

"Will you be okay here?" I ask.

"Of course. I'll be here when you return."

I nod. Finally, I head to the front door, but I linger, putting on my shoes in the foyer just out of sight to watch him for a while.

From what I see, Sephtis seems to be gathering his bearings.

"Please, let me do this for her." He says to himself aloud, he takes a deep breath approaching my traumatized pet cat slowly. "Okay Muffins," He says, facing Mr. Muffins. "I have a band-aid and a kiss from the wife. Bring it on."

He kneels down and starts to work the webbing from Mr. Muffin's limbs; he's surprisingly...gentle, as I watch from afar. I feel a blush crawl up my cheeks.

The minute Mr. Muffins is free, he gives a single meow, leaps from the tile, and like a flash of orange lightning, bolts down the hall, I can't help but smile at his sense of self-preservation.

Satisfied, I head out the door without another word.

# RHIANNE

I know I'll barely make it to work on time today, but all things considered, it's worth it.

I peer in the side-view mirror of my car— it had miraculously reappeared in my driveway, whereas Gary's car had vanished without a trace. My own car now runs perfectly, unlike how it had been just last night. For a moment I almost wonder if everything that had happened yesterday was all a dream.

But there was definitely no denying what I'd seen and experienced the night before, nor that intense kiss with Sephtis this morning. Heat rises to my cheeks. Sephtis is a lot different from what I'd imagined. He was unintentionally funny, gentle, and extremely sexy. It was difficult to imagine that this was the same Sephtis I saw in the woods. The skeletal remains that lay strewn across the pit I'd met him in remain in the back of my mind—along with the ease with which he killed Gary. It makes a chill run down my spine. He'd been nightmare fuel then, but today I feel like I'm crushing on him like a schoolgirl.

*I must be going out of my damn mind.*

Despite the way Sephtis comes across now, I know that a darkness looms there, and though he'd spared me last night, could I truly *trust* him?

As my office looms ahead, I think: *That's a problem for after work.*

I need to get my head in the game, or else I wouldn't be able to feign ignorance of Gary's whereabouts.

Entering the Visionaries parking lot, my stomach drops at the chaos that surrounds me. A line of flashing police cars stretch around the building.

Inside, police officers and investigators are everywhere, and my coworkers frantically rush around the office floors. Documents are scattered about, and Gary's office is sealed off.

I'm immediately accosted by my co-worker and friend, Charlotte Alvarez, before I can reach my own office, she hands me a cup of coffee, "You missed the morning drama. The FBI came and seized everything from Gary's office. Apparently, they finally had enough evidence to prove that he'd been embezzling money from clients for years." She sucks her teeth, and shakes her head in disgust. "And, of course, he left us to take the fall. Asshole took the cash and got out of dodge before they could catch up with him."

"They think he went on the run?" I take a sip of coffee, grateful to have a distraction.

"They found his car at the airport, and there's surveillance of him boarding a flight to Mexico. From what I heard anyway, they won't tell us much about it..."

"The airport?"

"Yeah, can you believe it? Looks like he'd been planning this for a while. That's all I know, but personally, I think there's a lot more to this than what they're letting on."

"While they investigate it, will we be doing any work?" I ask, I doubt I can stay focused today, and with having worked overtime for so many days in the past few weeks, I'm ahead of schedule anyway. Though, I wonder if all the work I put in matters at all now.

Charlotte shakes her head again, causing her dyed bright red waves to bounce about her shoulders. "Not a damn thing. The partners are in a meeting, and we're supposed to sit tight, and make ourselves available for questioning..." She lowers her voice. "They asked to speak to you, Rhia."

My heart thunders in my chest, and I nearly drop my cup. "M-me?"

"Yeah. That one." She leans into me and nods at an agent whose back is turned to us. As if on cue, he turns and approaches us, and Charlotte excuses herself, leaving me to face the investigator alone.

"Are you Ms. Rhianne Summers?"

"Y-yes."

"Follow me."

I set the coffee down on a desk, and feel as though I'm on autopilot as I walk behind the suit. He leads me into Gary's office, then the agent closes the door, and the click of the lock echoes in my ears.

"Ms. Summers," He walks around the desk and plants his hands on its surface. "How well did you know Mr. Edwards?"

I level my voice as best I can, and say truthfully. "He's my boss, and we're friendly, but nothing more. Why do you ask?"

"This may be hard for you to hear, so it's better if I show you.. .searching through his files, we stumbled upon this one." Pressing a few keys on Gary's laptop, he clicks on an untitled folder and opens a slideshow of pictures.

I clamp my hands over my mouth, and I feel nauseous. Image after image of me in my bathroom are displayed, and myself in various other rooms in my house veiled only by my sheer curtains. I'm speechless, and sick to my stomach.

“Mr. Edwards is obsessed with you, Ms. Summers. There’s also surveillance of him tinkering with your car last night.” He shuts off the slideshow, and I'm grateful for it. “We’ve been after him for months now. I can tell you, ma’am, he is not the man everyone thinks he is. He’s done some horrible things that money allows a person to cover up. I know with every fiber in my being that not taking his offer for a ride saved your life last night.”

My eyes dart to him. “What do you mean?”

“We watched the surveillance in its entirety. We saw that Mr. Edwards attempted to lure you into his car, and you declined and walked away. Having your car towed instead was the right choice.” He folds his arms across his chest. “Ma’am, I know I’m not supposed to say this, but I truly believe something was looking out for you last night.”

Almost in a trance, I emerge from Gary’s office.

*What on Earth is happening?*

None of it makes sense, but Sephtis is the common denominator. Easing past my co-workers, I focus on getting to my office, but as I bump into a suited wall of muscle, I glance up and mutter a quick apology, and I move to make my way around it. Only my wrist is snatched before I can retreat, and I whirl around to come face to face with yet another colleague, this time, however, it's not a friendly face. Todd Chang stands before me, wearing a cruel smile.

“Sorry about that, Todd," I say, attempting to pull my hand back. "My mind is absolutely all over the place.”

“I guess so. I mean, with Gary gone, I’d be concerned about my job too,” he says, smirking. “I can’t imagine how stressful the realization must be that you have to start climbing the corporate ladder based on merit alone.”

I wrench my wrist back from him.

"Excuse me?" I reply in disgust, glowering at him. "I don't know what you're suggesting, but I got where I am based on my work ethic. The promotion that I earned, and you didn't deserve, is proof of that."

He glares back at me. "Gary isn't here to protect you anymore, so you should tread carefully."

"Or maybe you should," A voice issues from directly behind me, making each and every hair stand on end.

I whip around, and my jaw drops.

Sephtis's face is a visage of rage, his eyes both ice, and fire. Having arrived seemingly out of nowhere, he stands there, his presence seemingly larger than life, making Todd look like a tiny and insignificant creature, unaware of what is about to befall him. Yanking me behind himself, he takes a lethal step toward Todd.

"Better yet, how about you repeat what you just said to my wife?" Todd's eyes cross as he gawks at Sephtis, who looms over his smaller frame, like a predator with his prey. The lights in Visionaries buzz, their intensity increasing with every step Sephtis takes to close the distance.

# Sephtis

I hadn't intended to get into it with any of my Amata's co-workers, in fact, my intention had been to come and go without any of them taking notice of me. I'd wanted to bring Rhianne lunch, since something told me she'd go the day without eating. But she doesn't seem to be able to stop herself from getting into danger. My Amata is backed into a corner when she doesn't deserve to be. This man has no right to speak to her this way, and I can tell she's hurt by his cruel accusatory words.

As much as I want to blend in with Rhianne's peers for her sake, at this moment, I don't care about the world around me. I feel my fangs threatening to drop. With all the indignities she's had to face, here was yet another.

"I want you," I say, my voice reaching a deadly low, barely more than a whisper. "To repeat what you just said to my wife."

"I-I," Like the true coward he is, the man called Todd stammers, taking a step back with every step I take forward, glancing around at his fellow co-workers—no one dares to attempt to step in, they mind their business, as they should. And, we're well out of the view of the agents investigating Gary. Todd's eyes dart to Rhianne, and it enrages me that he should even set his gaze upon her. "L-look, I didn't know she was married." He finally blurts.

"Do I look like I give a fuck? Repeat what you said so that her husband might hear you." All I want to do is tear this human apart, it would be so easy. But as I start to get closer and closer to the man, Rhianne steps from behind me.

"Sephtis, there's too much madness happening here, and I don't feel well. Can you take me home?"

I know what she's thinking, I can see it in her eyes. She's afraid that she won't be able to get me to back off because once I truly start, I won't be able to stop. In part, she's correct. I'm a predator, an engine of war dedicated to the protection of my Amata against all enemies. And this man has crossed that line.

I turn to face her, my breath growing heavy and my eyes narrowed with rage. "After," I growl, and when I fix my gaze back on Todd, he nearly jumps.

"Please?" She whispers, she looks up at me and I see the desperate plea in her eyes as she clasps my forearm. "I want to go now...please, Sephtis. *Take me home.* "

In that instant something in me shifts. Her touch is like a drug, releasing into my veins and soothing my anger. Her face is so soft as she looks up at me, I can't help myself. I gently grasp her face and tip it up to mine before brushing a kiss across her lips. I breathe in and exhale her scent.

As much as it pains me to do so, I nod. "Of course," I coo, pulling her to me.

I lean into Todd one last time. "Let me make something abundantly clear to you...Be grateful. I spared you because it was Rhianne's wish, but if you ever disrespect her again, any thought of your fate you've ever had will pale compared to the one I'll ensure you receive."

Todd nods fervently, he has to know he's on the edge of his life, and that's enough for now.

With that, I kiss the top of Rhianne's head, grab her hand and pull her out of the building.

"Do you have your keys?" I ask her, "I'll drive you home."

She nods, pulling them out of her pocket. I take them with my free hand and open up the car door for her before getting into the driver's seat. I start the car up, but in the periphery of my vision, I see Rhianne tilting her head back. Her eyes are wet, and tears threaten to fall—though she refuses to let them.

"Rhianne..." I lean over in the driver's seat and pull her into my arms. She wraps her arms around my neck, and I just hold her for a moment, letting her regain her composure.

"I'm fine." She manages a smile. I gently wipe the tear that rolls down her cheek.

"I'll get you home," I say, pulling out onto the main road. After a moment of driving in silence, she shifts in her seat.

"How'd you even learn how to drive? Yesterday you didn't even know how the shower worked." Rhianne remarks from beside me.

"Remember, I told you I acclimate quickly," Is all I say, rolling smoothly to a stop at a red light. "Never mind that, I got you something."

I reach into the brown paper bag between us and lift out a Tupperware container like a prize. "Your favorite."

She makes a pleased sound and reaches for the box. Peeling off the lid, she hesitates.

"Avocado toast," I say. "You said it's something you liked, so I tried to remember it."

"This is an avocado and toast." She limply lifts out the slice of bread and an avocado half I'd lovingly packaged for her.

"Yes, Amata. Avocado toast." In the rearview mirror, I glance at her and frown. "I've done something wrong again."

Rhianne laughs, "This is not how—" I almost miss the next word because she's laughing so hard now. Her eyes are sparkling, and she keeps hiccuping with laughter. "—you make avocado toast!"

I frown at her suspiciously, but her laughter is contagious. Although I don't understand what's so funny, I can't help but smile. "How do you make it?"

"You mush it, then put it on toast, and the bread has to be toasted first." She makes a motion with her hands. "You know, like how they do it on those cooking shows."

I blink. "Cooking shows?"

Rhianne's laughter rings out like a bell. "Looks like you still got a lot to learn, and luckily you have me to teach you."

She leans her head against my shoulder for the rest of the drive, and suddenly, it's like nothing else exists. In that moment, I'm a happy husband.

# Rhianne

I give Sephtis a smile as I stand over the kitchen sink, washing my hands.

“No more screaming Mr. Muffins. Hm, does that mean the two of you are friends?" I ask, lending Sephtis my hand towel so he can dry his.

"I wouldn't say we're quite friends yet, but I think we've reached a mutual understanding."

"That's definitely progress," I say, and Sephtis lets out a chuckle of his own. He wraps an arm around my waist and pulls me near.

"Show me how you mush your avocados on toast." He says, looking at me with the smoldering gaze that has me melting every time. I slip around his side and lead him to the pantry.

Pulling a few slices of bread from it and placing them in the toaster, I smirk at him. "It's my specialty, I know it's not your usual thing, but I think you might like this too if you give it a try."

Sephtis watches intently as I peel the flesh from an avocado and begin to mash it up with my fork. As soon as it is ready, I smother the creamy avocado mixture over the hot slices of bread and sprinkle a dash of salt, fresh ground pepper, and a drizzle of olive oil on top for good measure.

"You really surprised me by showing up today. I also didn't know you knew how to drive or fix cars. Did you take the transit to get to my office? Does that mean you're acclimating more?" I can't help the flurry of questions I have for him.

Sephtis parts his lips, but I go on before he can speak.

"I'm realizing that I don't know much about you. Where are you from? What other powers do you have?... Were you going to use those powers on Todd?"

His silence makes the air in the room thicken, and I catch myself.

"Sorry for all the questions. I'm just really curious." I set a plate before Sephtis and another down for myself at the breakfast bar.

"Thank you, Amata," Sephtis says, but he sits at the bar with his jaw flexed.

I dig into my toast, and when he doesn't answer for a while, I look up at him.

"A part of me feels like I should have killed him," Sephtis says absentmindedly, lifting the slice of toast and studying it from all angles.

"No, you absolutely did the right thing backing down. That was Todd just being Todd. He's a pain in the ass, but he's harmless. He's just upset because I'm good at my job. He's had it out for me ever since I got my promotion and moved into the office he'd been eying for months." I shrug. "You can't kill everyone that says or does something to me you don't like."

"Yes, I can," he retorts, his tone deadly, putting the toast down. "That's something you need to learn fast. I can take a lot...I can tame my anger on my own behalf, but no one disrespects or hurts my wife. The next time, Amata, I will kill him." His eyes are hard, and when he says the words, it sends chills throughout my entire being.

“Right," I say, shifting my gaze from his.

“I’m sorry. It isn't my intention to frighten you, but I don't want to lie to you either.” His eyes blaze for a moment, then he releases a heavy puff of air and pushes his plate back toward me. "Eat the rest of this for me; I want to see to it that you are well-fed."

*He hasn't even taken a bite, he really is strictly carnivorous.*

I can only imagine how much he's been craving meat...and blood. When I used to eat meat, I had a few go-to dishes, I decide to myself that I'll pick a few things up for him from the deli when I order groceries again, and see what he takes to best.

"You never did answer my questions," I say, and Sephtis visibly tenses. "I barely know anything about you Sephtis..." I trail off, and he covers my hands with his own.

"Perhaps we should save that for another time."

"How can we even attempt to begin a relationship when we know nothing about each other? When I know nothing about you but your name?" I stare at our hands and frown, and the tone of my voice rises. "How can you say I'm your wife, your Amata, when you know nothing about me? I'm not asking for a life story, but you can at least tell me why you've been in that pit all this time, where you came from, and what you can do." I look up at him, straight into his eyes, and he's staring back at me with a guarded expression.

"No." He finally says, and I'm taken aback by him. I didn't expect him to fight me on this.

"No?" I ask, a bit shocked.

"No." He stands up, and I watch incredulously as he lifts my empty plate. "Rhianne, I trust my instincts, and believe me when I say: you are the one." He presses a quick kiss to my cheek before carrying my plate back over to the sink to wash it clean.

I can't help the warmth that spreads over my cheeks, and I'm torn by mixed feelings. On the one hand, I'm glad to see that he's trying to prove that he's not as vicious as he seems. He's been considerate and kind to me, not to mention he's the most gorgeous specimen of a man I've ever seen. On the other hand, I can't help but feel frustrated by his secretiveness.

I merely gaze at his back for a short while as he works, when an idea comes to mind.

“I appreciate that you are so protective of me," I begin. "And I also appreciate that you are trying to be the man I want you to be...especially considering I'm someone you don’t even seem to like,” I say, a wry smirk playing about my lips.

Sephtis turns, and arches his brow at me as he wipes his hands dry. “And where did you get the idea that I *don’t* like you?”

“Please,” I scoff, sliding off of the bar stool and striding slowly around the island. His eyes follow my every movement, and I have to admit that it does make me feel powerful to know that he's so captivated by me. I shoot him a mischievous look with a sultry stare beneath my lashes, and see his gaze blacken.

“Don’t think I forgot what you said in that pit in the woods: *‘You want nothing from me, except for me to leave. You have no interest in even eating me’.* Heck, you even chose Gary over me, but *I’m* of no interest? Way to add salt to the wound that is life.”

Sephtis stares at me for a moment. His eyes gleam with a trace of amusement when he looks at me, and I stifle a shiver of excitement. “Are you honestly telling me you’re offended that I spared your life? That makes no sense. Are we about to have our first fight?”

“No, we aren’t. I’m just communicating that I’m offended by your choice of words. You could have said that you were full, or made up some excuse, but nope, instead, you said you didn't want me, and bam, just destroyed my poor little heart."

"I don't think I can ever not want you, Rhianne..." He speaks and clasps his hands in front of him. "But, if you wish to speak of choices of words, maybe you should replay your request of me in your head."

I scrunch my face, and then my lips form a silent 'o'. "That is not what I meant."

"Perhaps, but it is what you said." He grins like the devil, and strides toward me slowly. "You want me to eat you, is that correct? Well, come over here, and I'd be happy to oblige. So be careful what you wish for, sweet Amata."

Something about his words makes my blood run hot and cold all at once. "That's not funny. You know I didn't mean it like that." I take a step back, but he slips an arm around my waist before I can retreat.

"I'm glad it's not funny to you because I'm not joking. Have you noticed that not once today have you corrected me in calling you my wife?"

My eyes widen as he draws me in. Sephtis's thumb brushes against my hip bone, and his eyes bore into me so intently I almost need to look away. Leaning down, he brings his lips inches from mine. "Does this mean you've grown fond of the idea of me being your husband?"

I gaze deep into his eyes, and I hear my heart hammering in my ears as a thrill heats my body. Slipping my arms around his neck, I hum, "Well, after seeing your escapades with Mr. Muffins, and your willingness to protect me...I might be willing to give the idea an honest thought..."

"Just a thought?" Sephtis growls, pulling me into his chest as his mouth descends onto mine. "What if I want more than just a thought?" He murmurs the words against my lips, and my legs nearly buckle.

I manage to pull back, though I yearn for his lips.

“I want to give us a chance...for something real...something serious,” I admit to him. "But I need to know more about you."

For a moment, I'm scared of what I might unleash with that statement. His eyes shift a bright shade of red, and a wickedly seductive smile curves his lips.

Snaking a hand into my hair, and tangling his fingers in my curls, he draws me into a deep kiss. I swear, my back arches in that moment as though someone has stuck a pin through me. His nails dig into my back, and I let out a muffled moan. He lets his hands slide lower, and he cups my ass cheeks and lifts, setting me on the countertop.

Positioning himself between my legs, his lips brush along my neck, and his breath is hot against my flesh.

“To answer one of your questions, I have an array of powers. For example..." He runs his tongue up my neck, and a moan bubbles up from deep inside my throat. “There is something quite special about my bite. Would you like me to show you?”

I nod wordlessly as my hands slide to his shirt, and I begin to fumble with the buttons. In a smooth motion, he divests himself of his shirt and tosses it aside. His body is perfectly sculpted. Rippling muscles and glowing skin covered in its curious lacework tattoo make my mouth water.

"Yes," I whisper, my voice weak. "Show me."

He begins to unbutton my blouse, his hands moving slowly and deliberately, taking their sweet time. I feel myself grow wet under his touch. He slides a hand inside my open blouse and trails hot kisses from my collarbone, up my neck. His tongue flicks out and strokes my skin.

He continues to kiss, sucking lightly, I pull him closer to me, and he makes a satisfied noise as he nips at my neck. I can feel the needle-pointed tips of his fangs graze my flesh, and I both revel and quake in the delicious feeling of massive anticipation. A moment later, his long fangs sink themselves deeply into my skin, the initial breach is shockingly painful, but just as suddenly, my eyes roll to the back of my head as an unexpected wave of pleasure overtakes me in a rush.

I gasp, growing wetter by the second. I can feel his venom seeping into my veins, spreading its heat throughout my body, my rapid heartbeat seems to make it spread faster. The warmth of his bite consumes me, and I can feel myself growing dizzy from the intoxicating pleasure of his deepest of kisses. I come hard, my inner walls pulsing. I hear myself moaning uncontrollably, and my hands grip his hair limply as I writhe beneath him. He holds me tighter than any man has ever held me, and I am lost in him, consumed with desire for this powerful, seductive creature that has me completely under his spell.

In that moment, there is nothing but us, locked in a fierce embrace of pleasure and desire. And as he draws his fangs from my skin at last, and drags his tongue along my neck, I know that nothing will be more thrilling, or more pleasurable, than being taken by this man.

My arms slump onto the counter, and Sephtis pulls away, sensually tracing bloodstained lips with his tongue, a smile plays at the corner of his mouth as he watches me.

I feel so relaxed, my breaths deepening, laboring. It's as though I'm sinking, sinking slowly into the most luxuriously comfortable bath from which I never want to emerge. The deepest massage has never gotten me to this state of relaxation, I feel boneless. Sephtis swims in my vision.

"What's...happening to me?" I ask in a mumble, fighting to keep my eyes open.

"The venom in my fangs is a powerful aphrodisiac, a little bit leaves my victims temporarily paralyzed in an orgasmic state, and entirely relaxed." He stops to stroke my cheek, brushing my hair out of my face. "It's an amusing way to subdue my prey. You'll still be able to see, to hear, to talk, to feel everything – but you won't be able to move or resist me. I'll be in total control, and you'll be forced to experience every inch of yourself begging for my touch. Every utterance, moan, or whimper of pleasure you make will only fuel my deep hunger for you...I can't help but find pleasure in how horrifying it must be to unwillingly enjoy dying." He says, his voice dark, and somehow more seductive than ever now.

The awareness of his words and the confusing feelings of arousal arise at the same time. My heart beats recklessly in my chest, but it's as he says, I'm helpless to do anything about it. The thought terrifies me, but the way he's saying it, like it's the most natural thing in the world, makes me feel conflicted--perhaps it's the venom, I get tingly all over hearing his voice alone like a caress on my raw nerves. I drag in a tremulous breath.

Holding me steady, he cups my face in his hand, his touch deliciously gentle, raising goosebumps all over my skin, and he looks me deep in my eyes. "The effects won't last long. I made sure of it. You can trust me, Rhianne, I would lay down my life before I ever hurt you."

My lips part and I can feel my body growing less and less responsive to my commands, but I had long since stopped even thinking of resisting his touch. I want to hate this feeling, but as I stare up at him, my body weak and craving for his caress, I am powerless to do it.

"I will not lay a finger on you until you beg me to." His voice is a low growl as he stares at me, his eyes do not waver.

I believe him. "What happens if I do?" My voice is so soft, dreamy, almost unrecognizable to myself.

He runs his hands down my body, and I respond to him like a puppet, electrified by the light stroke of his fingers, so eager for more.

"Then, I will do this..." he breathes, "and so much more." He leans down and whispers his seductive promise in my ear, "I will make you feel pleasure beyond anything you've ever felt before."

I pant beneath his touch, thinking about it for a moment. It's terrifying, but the thought of being safe in his hands, of being his, is...thrilling. My answer comes irresistibly: "Yes, please—"

Before I complete my answer, he's already raised a hand, and webbing shoots from one corner of the ceiling and its opposite. In quick succession, he lashes another silken band over the first, and weaves the other end around my wrists, carefully knotting the incredibly soft elastic rope to relieve my wrists of any pressure. I'm forced to lift my arms high above my head, as he pulls the wrist rope taut and knots another anchor. For something that feels so supple, so delicate, it's unimaginably strong. My legs follow, lifting my body so I am completely suspended in midair, snared and controlled by Sephtis. Finally, he hikes my skirt up to my waist, and easily yanks off my panties in a quick tear of fabric.

I feel so exposed and vulnerable. I can't move, can't resist. All I can do is feel while my wetness drips on the tile, my legs spread, my pussy open and vulnerable to him—for him.

He stands back to admire his handiwork, his eyes gleam with satisfaction as he marvels at me, his gaze flickering over every inch of my body with a hunger that makes me tremble.

His tongue slowly winds around the contours of his lips, fangs glinting sharply in the light. "You look absolutely delectable, Amata," he says, "You're mine, Rhianne. I will have you; you have no idea how much I wanted to take you, but only when you begged me for it, not a second before."

A moan escapes me as he trails his hands down my neck to my breasts, and massages them gently. He pulls down the cups of my bra and captures my tender nipple between his lips, sucking and nipping. I arch into him; he feels so good. Its twin receives the same treatment, and I can't stifle the moans coming from the back of my throat, a warm, wet sensation spreads slowly between my legs.

Pulling back, he hooks one hand beneath my knee and drags my pussy closer to him. A growl escapes his lips at the sight of my dripping arousal glistening on my own.

He runs a thumb along my slit, and the sensation of his finger skating along my wetness coaxes a shudder out of me. He brings it to his mouth, his tongue darts out, and he laps at it, groaning in satisfaction before hungrily sucking my essence off his fingertip. My body burns with need, he continues to lick, while I struggle helplessly, squirming against the webbing that binds me in place, my hips wanting to thrust towards his tongue, to feel it on my clit, to feel it everywhere. I only manage a pathetic bounce.

"Mmm, you are so delicious," he says huskily. "You taste even sweeter than I imagined. You're too addictive, Rhianne."

I clench again at the sound of my name on his lips.

"I'm going to claim you," he says, his voice a rumble, "I will take you, every inch of you, I won't stop until I've had my fill..."

A sense of tension, of desire, of longing, courses through me; all of my senses are heightened. I watch him, half in disbelief that this is actually happening. I'm hanging in his web, bound and completely at his mercy. Somehow, I'm ready for this. I'm ready to give myself to him completely.

He places my legs over his shoulders. I feel his mouth against my wet slit, and his tongue enters me, hot and wet. My juices mix with his saliva as he laves me.

"Sephtis— Aah—"I gasp brokenly.

"Say my name again." His voice is like velvet in my ears, his breath is hot against my slick folds.

"Sephtis..." I moan. "I want you."

I feel him draw back, and his teeth sink into my thigh. I let out a sharp gasp as he sucks on me. I shiver from the waist down and my center throbs in response. Everything tightens, and my shuddering breaths come in soft moans. I could almost cry.

I'm so hot for him, my sex is absolutely soaked with my wetness. I see his fangs streaked with my blood as he pulls away, and I feel his hands on my ass, his nails sinking almost painfully into the globes of my buttocks.

"You're very wet, Amata..." He purrs, and raises his gaze to my face, "And, so beautiful..."

His tongue traces my slit gently, teasingly, and then I feel him run it over my most sensitive, already throbbing flesh. I shut my eyes as he draws torturous circles around my clit, faster and faster. I tremble and moan, my head lolling back, my body so desperate for more, for anything at all.

He flicks his tongue against my clit over and over, each time more vigorously than before. My moans become more continuous, and I channel everything that I'm feeling into high-pitched, desperate cries.

He slides a finger in, and then another. I feel him thrusting them inside of me, scissoring his fingers inside my tightness, acting as a warm-up for his thick, hard manhood. I moan loudly as he works his finger against my spot, tightening around his digits. I want to cum, and I can't stop the way my body shakes from the overwhelming sensations.

"Oh—oh god—" I cry, and he yanks me closer in response, sucking hungrily on my sensitized, swollen clit. The room spins, and tears well in my eyes.

"Tell me you're mine," He says his voice a dark ripple, relishing the utter torment he's inflicting. I feel my leg muscles convulse, straining to break through the paralysis and wrap around him. He only presses his tongue harder. He pulls back only to hiss: "Say it," his voice hoarse and demanding.

He bites down on my clit and hot mascara tears pour down my face.

"I'm yours!" I scream as I come against his soft lips and wicked tongue, tightening around his fingers. As the first wave of pleasure tears through me, I cry out louder, my hips quivering with a frenzied passion. I feel my body contract with ecstasy, and my orgasm only grows stronger when he stiffens his tongue and flicks my clit quickly, without stopping, holding me rigid.

"I'm yours! I'm yours!—" I sob, and I gush onto his fingers. His greedy lips find my opening, and his tongue claims every drop.

Sephtis pulls me close and lays a kiss on my pussy, I throb against him, beyond all thought as he trails warm, wet kisses along my trembling thighs.

I can only pant as if I had just run a marathon. My core is aching; it's so empty, I want to feel him inside me again so badly—but this time, I need more of him. I feel my back arch when he lets out a soft purr. "And I am yours...so tell me what you want..."

My eyes are still shut, and I feel his hot breath on my wet slit. I want more, much more. I don't know how to say it, but he knows.

The loss of his touch is agony when he pulls away from my pussy, and I whimper in protest when he leaves me to hang limply in his bondage.

He moves his face to the side of mine and presses his lips to it, his lips dragging over the shell of my ear before he speaks. "Tell me what you want, Amata," he repeats, "and I will give you what you need."

I bite my lip and part my lips. "I...I need..." I whisper, "I need you inside me..."

He takes hold of both cheeks of my buttocks and lifts me, his grip biting into my skin.

His voice absolutely thick with desire, he whispers, "I'm going to fill you up so deeply with my cock, I won't stop until you beg me to, Rhianne." His words drip with passion, daring me to resist the pleasure that he promises. "I'm going to leave you aching for me...and only me."

A moan tumbles from my lips in response.

Gripping my hips firmly in both hands, he draws me to him until I'm in line with his swollen erection and I strain to spread my legs more to accommodate him. I gasp at the feel of his throbbing length, and my throat tightens with the fear that he won't fit. He's so hard, heat radiates off of him like a furnace. I shift my hips so he's pressing against my wetness and feel the answering pulse from his desire, teasing me, almost but not quite touching the epicenter of my longing. I whimper my frustration.

"Please..." I beg, "Seph—" He begins to bring my hips down onto him, his cock entering me, stretching me. I groan, overwhelmed by his size, he's so big...it's almost too much. And then he thrusts all the way into me, balls deep, to the hilt, and I wail.

"You're so tight..." He growls. I writhe against him, my arms and legs shaking, but I know he won't let me fall.

I let out a moan as I feel his throbbing member begin to pump in and out of me. He's slow at first, drawing out every single thrust for agonizing pleasure.

His grip tightens on the roundness of my ass, and I moan his name. He growls in response, thrusting inside of me with a heavy slap. He picks up the pace, pumping his cock inside of me, driving in and out of me with absolute ferocity—His balls slap against my ass each time and my cries of pleasure fill the room.

I feel myself being driven backward with the rhythmic force of his body slamming into me, my breasts bouncing with each pump. I strain against my restraints as he starts to move in a way that only he can, a way that soon drives me absolutely mad.

He thrusts his hips against me, grinding against my clit, and I feel myself tightening around him again, already begging for another orgasm.

I scream his name feeling him thrust hard into me. I don't know if he knows how much he's driving me crazy, how my body is already shaking with another climax, how he's only making it worse.

"Come for me, Amata," he growls. He thrusts harder, hitting my sweet spot with every plunge. He pushes himself into me, again and again, with inhuman strength and speed. I cry out in pleasure, my voice echoing through the room.

"I'm—I'm..." I moan, my legs are shaking again and my walls clench desperately against his shaft. He pulls my hips towards him crushing me against his body, he rolls his hips slowly so I feel him so deep inside, and his tongue plunges into my mouth as he fucks me. I moan against him, my body exploding into another hot, rushing orgasm. He moans into our kiss as he starts to thrust faster and faster, his rhythm never faltering.

My muscles contract spasmodically around his throbbing length, and a climax washes over me, every nerve in my body tingling with pleasure. I spill my juices onto his shaft as my inner walls clamp down and release around it, and finally break our kiss crying out his name over and over again.

"Rhianne...Amata..." He rasps, swelling and pulsing inside of me—sending me over the edge again, filling me up with hot ropes of his cum and my body welcomes his seed.

I can feel his heart pounding against my chest and the steady throb of his cock inside of me. He kisses me fervently, pulling back only to devour me with his hungry, red gaze.

"You're amazing..." He rumbles, his eyes aglow. "I can't get enough of you..."

He pushes back into me, hitting my sweet spot every time, pain weaving inextricably with pleasure. I'd beg for mercy if I could, but the only sounds I can manage are outcries and whimpers of unadulterated pleasure, my arms and legs shaking. I can feel yet another climax building inside me, like a tidal wave building power in the ocean.

He pumps his cock into me, I feel my pussy clenching uncontrollably around him, the next wave crashes into me, and I cry out his name. He groans into the crook of my neck, and I feel the hot spurts of his cum pulse against the walls of my core.

He pulls me close and wraps his arms around me, kissing my neck. I wriggle my wrists, wanting so desperately to hold him, but they're still bound, "Sephtis, I can't move..." I whisper dazedly, my heartbeat erratic.

He laughs softly in response, his arms tightening around me even more. I feel the points of his fangs at my neck. "I know..."

I close my eyes, a hot shudder running through me as his fangs slowly pierce my skin, my breath catching in my throat. I moan his name feeling him pulling me closer as his body seizes me in a vice-like grip. I feel his bite intensify—as if he's drinking from me, my veins pounding with the mixture of pleasure and hurt. Every tug of his lips drawing deeper pleasure from me. I moan louder, my pussy quivering against his cock.

"Sephtis..." I moan, "Oh fuck..."

His response is a deep guttural sound that sends a shiver down my spine. In a daze of desire, I murmur dreamily, breathlessly, “If this is how it feels...you can take all you want from me...”

Instead, I only hear him take in a sharp inhale and withdraw from me, leaving me weak, and spent.

I whimper as he runs his tongue soothingly along my neck. Letting out a long, satisfied sigh, my eyelids flutter closed; I feel as though I might pass out. My head is swimming with ecstasy, and I can't think. My body feels heavy and languid, and I'm utterly content. I almost forget that I'm hanging in the air, bound with silk, connected to him by his cock.

I look up lazily through my half-closed eyelids, and I see him staring down at me with awe and wonder, but also an intensity that makes my heart race, his eyes glowing red with appetite. His fangs are streaked with my blood, and his lips kiss swollen and stained red. I can see the lust in his eyes, and feel the way his cock is still hard, throbbing, begging for more. He's struggling to control himself, to keep from drinking more, and I know he's worried about me. I tremble at the sensation of him slipping out from deep within me, my wetness and his seed tracing a warm trail down my thighs.

Sephtis releases me from his bondage, catching me just as I collapse. I can see the conflict in his eyes, in his expression. He's holding himself back, his lust and his concern battling it out in his mind. I lift my head, my lips brushing against his, and my next words make his eyes widen.

"I want you..." I murmur. My voice is weak and hoarse, my body aching from him, and for him, and I can't stop trembling. He closes his eyes and groans, a long shuddering breath ripples through his body.

He lifts me bridal style, and kisses my eyelids, before carrying me to the couch in the living room.

I'm set down with such gentleness, enveloped in warmth and comfort, cocooned by the blanket Sephtis has wrapped around me. He takes his time affectionately tucking me in.

His venom still has my body heavy and my mind locked in a fog, and his lips brush a tender kiss against my cheek.

"It's been a long day...Relax, Amata, I am so proud of you," he turns on the television, and flicks through the channels, "Just tell me when, we can watch whatever you like."

My scowl finally catches his eye.

"What is it?" He tilts his head in question.

"You're a jerk, you know that?"

He chuckles, pressing his lips softly to mine, "I know."

He snuggles me close and turns his attention back to the screen and I can't help melting into his embrace as I struggle to regulate my breathing. My body is still aching, but he feels so right.

# Sephtis

"Sephtis..." Rhianne's voice seeps into my subconsciousness. Her voice is soft and gentle, a melody of whispers. "Seph, wake up—"

Sometime after, I feel Rhianne shaking my shoulder, I startle awake with a sharp inhale, Rhianne leans over me, her eyes are a warm, chestnut brown, with a hint of moisture in her lashes. Waking up to her beautiful face melts my heart, perhaps I didn't realize it until I see her reflecting the care I have for her back to me like a mirror.

In the bright light of the room, I can see that she's no longer tired and has changed into a form-hugging t-shirt and shorts. Drowsily, I lift a hand up to cup the perfect, radiant face of my sweet Amata, she's smooth and yielding in my hold. She smiles and holds me there for a moment, before shifting her face from under my palm and squeezing her slender fingers around my hand.

My gaze dips to see that her throat is now marred with my brand, dark bruises are already forming under the indentations of my fangs. My lust had overcome my better judgment, I had been an animal. Seeing my own markings so prominent brought both a perverse thrill and an even deeper remorse over what I had done. Within their darkness, I can see myself.

By the looks of it, she's showered, changed, and eaten. A sweet scent of her natural fragrance mingles with soap, jasmine water, and powder. The sweet and sultry scent makes me crave her even more. She leans in closer. I breathe in deep, my heart quickens, and my cock goes rigid against my thigh; her proximity alone is enough to make my fangs lengthen in my mouth.

"What time is it?" I mumble trying to keep the edge out of my voice.

"It's a little after ten now..." Rhianne answers and I can see the question in her eyes. "You've been sleeping for a while—I mean, I've been pretty noisy, but you slept through it all. Are you alright?"

"I just...must have been more tired than I thought." I sit up, averting my gaze from hers.

"You don't look so good, and you haven't eaten all day." She bites the fullness of her bottom lip, and my eyes are drawn to her mouth. "Is there anything I can do?"

My gaze snaps back to hers, I feel magnetized to her with an innate force, a need so visceral that I shudder. It's a hunger that no amount of food or drink can satisfy. I want her more than my next breath, more than anything in this world or any other. In every way imaginable.

I long to pull her close, instead, I pull my hand away swiftly, resisting the urge to draw her in and breathe in deeply of her intoxicatingly sweet scent, to do something I'd never be able to forgive myself for.

"I'm fine," I say more sharply than I intended. I see her recoil, and I hate myself for it, but I need to put some distance between us. Gentler now, I go on, "I don't need to eat every day, Amata."

It's the truth, but it still doesn't mean I don't need to eat soon.

"Okay..." She whispers.

I shake my head. I can sense her deep confusion and concern, but I don't have time to explain things to her right now. "That's thoughtful of you, but honestly, I just need more rest. I should turn in for the night ." I move to my feet, and press a brief kiss on her forehea d. "Goodnight, Amata."

She smiles, though it doesn't quite reach her eyes. She's worried. "Well, then get some rest. Goodnight—"

I don't let her finish, I can't. If I stay here any longer, I feel like I won't be able to resist the temptation of her. And if I give into my hunger, she'll be in danger. I work overtime to maintain my steady pace, I can feel her eyes on me as I head for the stairs.

Shutting the bedroom door behind me, I collapse onto the bed in a heap, and draw my knees to my chest. A cold sweat coats my flesh and soaks my clothes through.

I was foolish to think I could hold onto my control and continue this relationship with her despite my nature. Even more foolish to think I could resist her.

My hunger is killing me, and having her so close to me only makes it worse. The taste of her on my tongue, the smell of her body in my nostrils, it's enough to drive me to the brink of insanity. If I don't find a way to contain myself, Rhianne will wind up hurt. She will be at my mercy, and after a long period of suppressing my appetite, I will have no mercy in me for her. And that is a risk I cannot allow myself to take. I didn't think it was possible to want her so much, to need her so much. I'm pulled in every direction, unraveling, tormented by her proximity and her absence.

The pangs of hunger radiate throughout my entire being. I wrap my arms around my waist and grit my teeth through the sharp pains that cramp my stomach like a vice.

I pray Rhianne won't hear its growl.

*Please...be merciful...*

The pain spreads outward from my torso to every limb, and wracks every cell in my body, as every nerve arcs with electricity, consuming my entirety.

It is agony.

Finally, I allow the merciful darkness of unconsciousness to bring me relief.

# Rhianne

"Oh! Good morning," I greet Sephtis as I enter the kitchen. I'm surprised he's already up and about—considering he didn't seem to be doing all too well yesterday.

"Morning," He mumbles from the kitchen counter, turning to me, and smiling a little sadly.

I start towards him for a kiss, but he quickly nods to the table before I can reach him.

"I made breakfast."

I arch an eyebrow, and he lets out a small laugh. "And, no. I did not catch anything. I heard you the first time."

I turn to see a plate filled with a stack of pancakes with a garnishing of fresh fruit, and a glass of orange juice.

"You made all this?" I ask, surprised.

He nods. "I'm no chef, but I might have picked up something from your cooking shows. Sit down and I'll grab you some coffee."

I can't help but smile, as I take a seat at the breakfast table. "You're spoiling me."

"It's the least I can do. It makes me happy to provide for you." He says, not looking at me. I don't bother asking if he slept well, it's obvious he hadn't. He doesn't look good, but he looks better than he did last night. That doesn't mean he's recovered though. He's obviously still fighting something. Weariness is written all over his features, I can see the dark circles under his eyes.

I drizzle syrup onto a pancake and cut a triangle out of it, then try it, it's so warm, surprisingly fluffy, and melts in my mouth. "Seph, these are delicious!"

"Good. You deserve it." He pours steaming coffee from a carafe into my mug and sets it beside me.

"H-how are you feeling today? Did you sleep at all?" I venture, tentative, as I stir a sugar cube into my coffee.

He looks me in the eye. "I'll survive, Amata. Do not worry your pretty little head."

He looks up and gives me a quick smile, and I'm relieved that it's genuine, but I can't help but notice his fangs are longer than normal.

His eyes are darker than usual, his mannerisms more guarded. Yesterday, he went to bed after barely uttering a goodnight, and today he appeared physically better (slightly), but he clearly isn't mentally.

He seems to have noticed me noticing. His gaze grows darker, more intense. He swiftly returns to the kitchen to retrieve a mug of his own.

I can feel my face heating up at the thought that my gaze had been too obvious. I look away from him.

Something happened last night.

I can feel it in the way he holds me at a distance. It has to do with our moment of passion. I know it. I feel it like a hole, a gaping hole in the center of my chest. I feel it in my heart. I don't know how to process it, or what to do about it; I just know that I don't like it. It hurts.

*I wonder if I did something wrong?*

I've been trying to be mindful of giving him the space he needs. I twist in my chair and glance at the clock on the wall, I'm running late.

"Shoot! I'm going to have to run if I'm going to make it on time today. Thanks again for making breakfast."

Sephtis nods. "You're welcome. Leave your plate, I'll wash up."

I stand up from the table, grab my bag from the chair, and make my way to the door.

"Thanks again Sephtis; I'll be back in the evening," I say, standing on the front door's threshold, still, Sephtis keeps his distance.

"I'll be here, I'll feed Muffins while you're gone," he replies, his tone distant and monotone. "Drive safe out there, and have a good day at work, Amata. Tell me if Todd gives you any more trouble."

"He'd be a fool to try anything after what you said to him." I can't help but smile and chuckle lightly, as I turn to leave. "But, I will."

"...Amata?" I turn back to see him with a forlorn look on his face. "I love you."

I'm shocked by the sudden declaration and freeze on the spot, but I can't help but feel my heart swell. I open my mouth to respond, but he cuts me off.

"Don't say it back, not until you mean it. But I will spend my entire life proving it to you."

I nod, trying to contain the jumble of emotions swirling up inside. I want to say it back, so badly, but I'm not ready to say the words just yet. My heart feels something profound for him, I'm just not sure it's love yet. Especially so soon. How can I trust it? Eventually, all I can manage is, "I'll miss you."

I don't stick around to see his reaction, I hurry down the path, duck into my car, and pull out onto the road.

Since our moment together, Sephtis has become distant. Everything had been so intimate, so intense, but all of a sudden, he went cold. I'm not sure what to make of it, but he hasn't seemed to be his usual self ever since. But then, out of nowhere, he says he loves me? It's a lot to take in. I wish I had more time to process it. If I'm honest, I'm scared to return his feelings.

At work, I do my best to keep my worries at bay, and my head in the game. But it's not easy; I go through the day distracted and overthinking. I'm not even sure why I am so worried. Despite my best efforts, I'm practically on edge by the time evening comes.

Returning home from a long workday, I'm so caught up, that I hardly notice the new, but subtle difference in the atmosphere.

"I've been waiting for you to get home," Sephtis says as I walk in through the door. He captures me in a hug, and his lips press against mine. The kiss is deep, and passionate, his hands rove over my body. I'm taken aback, I wasn't expecting this. It's another 180-degree turn, something so intimate when he's been so distant.

He pulls me towards him so my body is pressed tight against his, and my arms wrap around his neck for support. His hands move to my thighs and he hoists me off the ground and squeezes me against him.

"How was your day?" He pulls back and smiles, and my heart skips a beat.

# Rhianne

"It was okay." Pulling away, and sliding down, I look at him. His eyes are a little brighter, but there is still something different about him. He looks happy, but still weary. "You seem to be feeling a bit better."

"A lot better, actually." He tightens his grip on my hips and presses another kiss to my lips. "I missed you, Amata."

"You did? I missed you too. I didn't realize how much until I got home and saw you."

We are smiling at each other now, he pulls me closer, and he leans down to kiss me again. He feels so solid and strong against me, it's difficult to remember that anything was ever wrong at all. We stay this way for a while, I can feel his heart thumping against mine, pulsing a rapid tempo as if it was aligning with my own. Suddenly and unexpectedly, our hearts are beating as one.

"Well, how was your day?" I say.

"It was quite unremarkable. But look," He points to Mr. Muffins, ensconced on the couch playing intently with a ball of eerily glimmering silk. "It seems, Muffins and I are the best of friends now." He smiles, lopsided and playful. There is a lightness I haven't seen in him in a while.

I chew the side of my bottom lip, and he rubs my shoulders.

“I’m fine, I promise. I know you’ve been worried, but everything is okay. I think the transition just hit me a little harder than expected.” He assures me. "Maybe, in the end, all I needed was some fresh air."

“Really?” I ask, and he chuckles as he takes my coat from me and hangs it up.

“Yes, really. Guess what? I made you something.” he calls back as he walks towards the kitchen.

I take off my shoes and set them by the door, then make my way down the hall after Sephtis.

"You made something else?" I hear the plates clink as he sets them down.

"Well, I burnt something, but garlic took out the taste of that...hopefully." Taking my hand, he escorts me over to the dining room table. “Come, sit,” he says.

Sitting down, I suddenly notice the *"Kiss The Chef"* apron he is wearing. I giggle. “Someone went shopping.”

“Well, as appreciative as I am for your brother’s clothing, I think I should have my own things."

The dish ends up being a simple but delicious spaghetti, and my stomach rumbles in appreciation as he sets the portion in front of me. The spaghetti is a swirl of al dente noodles, coated with vibrant red tomato sauce, with flecks of diced garlic throughout, lightly sprinkled with freshly grated parmesan cheese, and on top is a generous helping of finely chopped basil leaves that add a bright green burst of flavor.

I stare at it in awe at first, “Grocery shopping too?”

“And completely vegetarian,” Sephtis says. “Go ahead, try it.”

I dig in, and it's so delicious. It wasn't an elaborate meal and I didn't expect it to be; it's comfort food, so there are no frills, but it's perfect. "I'm really impressed." I say "This is really good."

He shrugs. "Well, I had a little help."

"From who?" I ask, and he leans over and kisses me. His lips are soft, and he smells fantastic. He always smells delicious, it's part of what I love about him, and I breathe him in.

"Muffins helped me." He looks so adorable, and I can't help but laugh.

"He did?"

"He kept me company," he replies, and he tucks a strand of his hair behind his ear, before lifting a bottle of Montepulciano red wine and pouring it liberally into the bell of my wine glass. He takes a seat beside me.

"That's too cute." I haven't seen Sephtis this at ease in a while. I didn't realize just how much I missed this side of him; everything about him is more relaxed, more open.

"Oh? Am I back to being cute now?" He arches a brow, with a teasing smirk.

"You're always cute..." I say taking a deep sip. "Well, until you're sexy."

"And what about handsome?" He ices me with his gaze, his arm snaking around the back of my chair.

I can't help it; I laugh. "Oh my God, you're ridiculous." But I feel my face heat up in a deep blush, and a stirring within me like a thousand fluttering wings.

He leans in, and kisses me again.

"Mmmm." Kissing him back, all my worries melt away as the warmth radiates through our embrace, the comfort from a simple home-cooked meal and the buzz of wine blend in a perfect symphony of happiness, and desire.

"I have something you might just appreciate. I'll be right back." He disappears into the hall, headed for the powder room, and I can hear a bit of commotion. This has me extremely curious. Emerging after a while, he reappears, crosses one leg over the other, and leans against the kitchen's entryway. "The saleswoman said I could be a model, but I think it was just to get me to overspend. Although, I do care about one person's opinion. Does the wife approve?"

My jaw goes slack, "She was right. You look really handsome."

He does. He always had, but this new look has me frozen in awe.

The white-collared shirt he wears has two buttons undone at the top and shows hints of the black tattoos, lacing his skin. His navy blue herringbone suit jacket, paired with the matching slack, are both tailored to perfection. His hair is pulled back into a loose ponytail, with his forelocks framing his face in a way that almost begged for me to run my fingers through it. He manages to still look attractive as ever dark circles and all--in fact, it gives him a sort of gothic bent. It's a look that'd make any woman stop in their tracks, and I certainly don't mind being that woman.

"You're staring, Amata," he says as he adjusts his cufflinks.

I avert my eyes, another flush creeping over my cheeks anew, and momentarily at a loss for words. "Sorry. You just look really nice. I'm not used to seeing you dress up like this." I look him over again, taking in his every detail.

"Neither am I, but it feels good. And I'm so glad that you have given your approval." He winks. "Besides, when I stand next to you, I shouldn't look like a bum next to a queen. Wouldn't you agree?"

I giggle. "No, I don't think so."

I swallow hard. I'm actually feeling extremely flustered by him. I've never seen him like this before. He looks impeccable and quite princely even. His dark eyes slowly travel down my body, making me feel naked.

"What's more, I want to see you in this..." He bends reaching for a shopping bag on the ground. "Just so I can peel you out of it."

He hands it to me and I'm visibly shaking as I pull out the most beautiful dress I've ever seen. I'd never gotten a chance to even think about getting something so extravagant for myself. It's a deep, silky midnight blue, one-shoulder, sheath.

I can see the genuine appreciation for me in his eyes, I can also see the hunger in his gaze. "Do you want to try it on?"

I nod, and I go off to the bathroom to change. I can feel the heat rising in my cheeks and my chest. I can feel the blood rushing through my veins. It fits like a glove, made just for me. When did he have time to get this?

"Sephtis?" I say, as I step out into the hall, I notice mood music being played from the living room.

"Follow my voice, Amata."

I walk in the direction of his voice, and the sweet, soft music, and when I do, I'm greeted by the sight of him just finishing lighting a candle. He straightens, upon seeing me, a distinct hunger in them makes them glow deep red.

"Turn around." He commands, his voice a rumble, and I do.

My knees shake slightly as I twirl for him. "How do I look?"

A low growl escapes his lips. "You look like an angel." He rakes his eyes over me from head to toe. He holds his hand out, and I step into it. He takes my hand and kisses it. "You are beyond beautiful. On the inside and out."

"Thank you, Sephtis, for everything."

"I really mean it, Rhianne. You've been so kind to me. It's only been a few days, but I feel very connected to you. And the way you look at me...has become one of my favorite things to see...Will you dance with me?"

I'm surprised by the request, but I nod.

He wraps me in his arms, and I rest my head on his shoulder. Swaying me gently, he hums the soft music.

"Sephtis?"

"Yes?"

I look up into his eyes.

*I need to ask him.*

The new clothes, Gary, Sephtis's aversion to any human food, his cocoon-lined pit, and his sudden mood change...it's all coming back, to overshadow what should have been a beautiful moment. I can't help but tremble in his hold—and he notices.

"Amata, what is it?" He asks, "You're shaking..." He pulls back to look me in the eyes. "Are you cold? Is it something I did?"

I part my lips, but the words won't come out. As I continue to look at the most beautiful man I've ever met, I realize several things I'd been too afraid to say, but I can only give voice to one.

Giving him a small smile, I reach up and caress the side of his face. "I've grown very connected to you, too. I'm falling for you. How are you doing it? How are you making me feel this way?"

His eyes light up. "Amata."

He takes my lips with his, and I melt in his hold. I breathe him in, and when he kisses me, it feels like the first time all over again. It's soft and sweet and full of passion. I can feel myself falling into him, and I don't want it to end. I kiss him back, and I'm feeling more alive than I have been in weeks. I feel happy for the first time, and I know that I'm right where I belong. I'm home. I'm his home.

"That makes me very happy to hear," he says in a purr. He lowers his lips to my neck, I feel his breath on my skin and his arousal stirs against me, pressing against my stomach and my body responds. I can't help the lustful moan that escapes my lips. His tongue flicks the spot on my neck below my ear, and I shiver. I move in closer to him, and he is still humming softly in my ear, but I need more. I need him to make me feel like I'm the only woman alive. I feel like I'm going to melt in his arms.

Pulling away from me, he pushes a hand through his hair. "Let's clean up, and if you're not too tired, maybe we could watch a movie and spend time together."

"I'm not too tired."

"Good. We can watch anything you'd like—"

I step into him. "That's not what I meant," I say and draw him back towards me, connecting our lips again, he groans when I slip my tongue into his mouth. I run my hands down his front, feeling every muscle of his powerful body. He pulls me closer, and I can feel his arousal pressing into my stomach.

Sephtis hoists me up hiking up my dress in the process, and I lock my legs around his waist.

"I need you in my bed." I gasp.

***

He kicks the door closed behind him, as I grind against his hardened, pulsing manhood.

"Put me down," I breathe a sultry whisper into his ear. Lowered to the ground, I sink to my knees before him and tug at his pants. I undo the button of his fly, pull the zipper tag down, and smirk at his boxer briefs; within them, his erection strains.

"I love the view from here," I tell him, brushing the tip with my fingers and watching it twitch.

"I agree. You look very good on your knees, Rhianne," He tells me breathily with a slow smile as his hands find my hair and fists it into a tight bundle.

I bite my lip glancing up at him, but I don't take him into my mouth yet. I slip my hands around his massive cock stroking him slowly, feeling the soft velvet skin covering the steel beneath. His muscles contract with every stroke, and I want them to tense, I want to know I'm doing it right. I want him to tremble, to shake, to explode before me. Slowly pumping it as I look up at him, I see hunger and desire burning in his gaze.

"Rhianne," He whispers my name in a tortured growl, as though it pains him to speak. I hear the desire in his voice, he closes his eyes, and I know he wants it as badly as I do.

"Do you want me to lick it?" I ask breathlessly looking up at him, and his jaw clenches. With a nod he opens his eyes and the lust in them blinds me for a moment. So I do, I lick the tip, tasting him. A low groan comes from deep within his chest, and I smile. Running my tongue up the underside of his shaft to the head, I lick him like an ice cream cone, and he tastes divine. Sucking him into my mouth, I pull him in as deep as I can go. He pushes his hips toward me, to get more of his cock in—there's just so much of him, but I'm eager to take him in as far as I can. He hits the back of my throat, and I bring my hands up, holding his ass in my hands, and he tightens his grip on my hair, pulling me in. I continue to suck and swirl my tongue around his cock, taking him in as he'll go. His hands are gripped tightly in my hair and he begins to thrust his hips, forcing himself deeper and deeper into my mouth, breaching my throat.

"God, Rhianne—" he groans, a deep growl rumbling in his chest. The vibrations set my entire body trembling. I want him more than anything right now, but I want to make him lose control first. He's panting heavily, eyes closed tight as he gives himself over to the pleasure radiating between his legs.

"That feels so good..." He grits through clenched teeth, his voice straining when I slurp along his length. His body becomes rigid, and he stills. The sudden tension in his body sends me into a frenzy. I want him to lose control. I want his release so badly. He grunts again, and I know he's about to cum. I want it, I want all of it. I want him to fill my mouth with his cum, to show me what he's made of, to show me how much he wants me.

"That's enough." he pulls free from my mouth, throwing me for a loop.

I look up at him, and he meets my gaze, fire in his eyes. I'm hot, I'm ready, and now I'm confused. Standing in front of me, his cock still hard, he grabs my hands and pulls me up to my feet. He's breathing heavily; with hooded eyes gleaming red, he stares down at me, his chest heaving.

"Amata, I need you." He pulls me close, running his hands up my sides and cupping my breasts. "Pull off your dress, before I rip it off you," he growls.

In an instant, I step back and wriggle out of my dress, standing before him in nothing but a set of lacy black undergarments. He looks at me with hungry eyes and then he's on me, pushing me back onto the bed, pulling off my bra, and sucking on my nipples until they're hard, aching, swollen peaks. I arch into him with a mewl, the teasing becoming unbearable. Sephtis maneuvers his way between my thighs, and his mouth moves lower, kissing down my stomach to the waistband of my panties. I pull him closer, my fingers running through his hair. Suddenly, he grabs my wrists in a hand and pulls them over my head.

I can only grind against him, my head thrown back into my satin pillows, "Please!" I whisper, and he winds silvery bands of silk webbing around my wrists binding them to the headboard. I look at my bound wrists and I tug on the silk ropes. It's tight and strong, I can't break free. I can't move as he looks at me with a darkly seductive fanged smile.

"I like you tied up, Rhianne." He says, and I close my eyes and writhe against him.

I'm cold in my near nudeness, but Sephtis is hot. His body warms mine even before his hands do, his heat radiates from him like a furnace as he looms over me. I melt against him as his mouth trails a path of heat down my stomach. He plants a kiss on the waistband of my underwear and I tug on the silk ropes in frustration.

"I want you inside me so bad," I gasp, and he chuckles.

"I know you do. I can feel it..." He slips a finger between my slick lips through my panties. That single finger slides up and down, wetting my panties with my fluid. In a smooth motion, he pulls them off me and lets my thong drip onto the floor. "You're so soft, so hot, so wet, so slick..." he moans. "Spread your legs wider for me, Amata."

Panting with need, my legs open for him, the cool air hitting my wet pussy. He doesn't touch me yet, instead, Sephtis's hands make their way to my thighs, spreading me even more. He runs his hands down my legs, rubbing his rough hands along the tender flesh of my calves. He takes my ankles, binding one then the other and tying both to each post at the footboard, like he has my wrists.

I need him. The anticipation is too much.

“Please,” I gasp, desperate to feel him inside me, and frustrated that I can't do anything about it. I call his name, but it comes out in a whimper.

"Soon, Amata." He breathes back. Sephtis's scorching gaze is on me now as he watches me squirm, staring at me like he wants to devour me alive.

Vulnerable, and spread, my legs begin to tremble, my body tensing with anticipation. Slowly and deliberately, he moves between my thighs. Now, I can feel the weeping head of his erection straining against my sensitive, swollen lips, pulsing there with every beat of his heart. A tingling sensation roars through me, the heat of my flow rising from deep inside me, my entire body breaks out in goosebumps. Sephtis rubs up and down along my slick folds in teasing strokes, slipping along my clit, sending electricity through my entire body, torturing me until I beg him to take me.

“Please...I can’t take it anymore.”

All of a sudden, he's there. With little warning, he sheathes all of himself in me, in one long, deep thrust forward and his eyes redden. I cry out as his massive cock slams into me. I hadn't been prepared for the rush of pleasure that crashes over me like a breaker on the shoreline. He powers into my body, again and again, fucking me so hard that it almost hurts. My cries are silenced by his mouth, but I can't contain them; my body feels so good, I feel so full of him that I can't stop.

"Mmh, you feel incredible,” he grunts through clenched teeth. He strokes at an agonizingly slow pace, pulling almost all the way out before forcefully burying himself inside of me again and again. His lips find my neck, his tongue laving the length of my throat, putting a deliciously searing heat and achy pressure on the place where he'd marked me with a passionate bite the day before. I feel my walls clench around him, afraid to let him go.

"Does it feel good, Amata?" he asks huskily.

Sephtis moves both of us slowly together, sliding in and out of me like we are moving as just one being — two halves that become whole again simply by joining in this way once more. It's almost impossible how easily our bodies fit together and how effortless it is to slip back into perfect sync with him.

“Yesss—” I whisper in response, my eyes rolling back.

I moan again, and he picks up his pace, pounding into me with a controlled ferocity that only heightens the pleasure. Each stroke sends shockwaves of pleasure through my body. My walls clench tightly around him as he moves faster and deeper.

"Look at me, Amata," he commands me. He grips my waist and holds me still as he thrusts heavily into me, his pace so passionate that it's almost painful.

I do as he says, gasping for breath. He moves at an ungodly pace and all I can do is cry out from pleasure as he drives into me.

“Yes,” he hisses, leaving a trail of soft biting kisses down my neck to my chest, and takes one hard nipple into his mouth while he continues to slide powerfully inside of me. His breath on my bare skin sends chills racing up and down my spine. My body is on fire; every nerve in me feels electrified with unbridled desire for him as every muscle in my body trembles from the effort it takes not to come undone at any moment from sheer blissful rapture. It's almost too much but it feels so good, each time better than before— an overload of sensation that overrides all rational thought until there's nothing left but the pure instinct to fuck more desperately, more intensely—

But I want to feel him sink his fangs into me, and fill me with his sweet ambrosia of pure ecstasy. To have him suck my blood as he fills me with his seed.

"Your venom..." I pant, exposing my neck more for him. I yearn for his bite, I want to feel his fangs slide into my body. Gripping into the comforter beneath us, he slams into me. I cry out. "Do it...I want it..." I beg. "Drink from—"

I can feel every muscle in his body tense as he pulls me to him and I scream out in pleasure. He hits just the right spot at just the right angle and I collapse beneath him as wave after wave of undulating pleasure washes over me. The feeling is so intense that I see stars. I want him to bite me, but it never comes; instead, my orgasm tears through me, and my back arches as I feel myself come completely undone in his arms. My sex convulses against his girth, he slams into me harder and pulls my neck to him, his other arm wrapped around me. I can feel the heat of his breath on my throat, I thrill beneath the grip of his hand. He's panting hard, his hold so tight around me.

"Amata, don't make me-" he rasps, his voice coarse with restraint.

"Make...you...what?" I ask between labored breaths, but it's too late. He pulls himself out of me, and I feel the loss of him instantly.

I'm not done; I want more. I whimper, and he stares at me, his gaze dark and glowing red like hot coals.

"I want more," I beg, breathless and frustrated. He knows what I want, I can see it in his eyes, he's in my head. Instead, I'm left to lie on the bed, satisfied but unsatisfied. I've just been having the best fuck of my life, and he refuses to finish me off. His chest rises and falls rapidly, his breath coming in short, ragged gasps.

This afterglow is less than sweet.

"What the hell just happened?" I ask. I want to sit up, but I can't because his silk is still tight around my wrists.

He looks at me, like he's fighting something in himself, and takes a shaky breath. "Rhianne, I just can't—" He says, and then he stares at the ceiling and runs a hand over his face.

I can feel my pulse pounding in my temples, and I begin to struggle against my restraints.

"I'm sorry." He says, his voice soft, sincere.

And as much as I want to be, I can't be mad when he looks at me the way he does. He unties my ankles. I close my eyes, as he straddles me and unties the bindings from my wrists, then presses a quick kiss against my lips, then forehead before he climbs off me.

"It's fine," I say, I roll over in my bed to face him. "Just tell me what's wrong?"

"It's just—I think I may have overdone it for tonight." He sits up, his back to me, and runs his fingers through his hair.

My brow furrows as I consider him, his posture stiff, looking both troubled and guilt ridden.

"Seph—" I move to touch him on the shoulder, but he's already gotten up, retrieving his shirt from the ground with him.

“I'm going to turn in early. I will see you in the morning, Amata. Remember, I love you...no matter what.” He tells me, and I can feel his regret. He gives me a swift peck on the lips, and he sweeps out of the room before I can even respond.

I can't help but utter, "I love you too." The words whisper out of my mouth as I sit up on the bed, but only reach an empty door frame. And I remain there for a long while, still trying to catch my breath, confused.

# SEPHTIS

I take my time shakily getting into the shower, then stand under the stream of hot water and go over the night's events in my mind. Rhianne, she is amazing, beyond anything I've ever imagined. The most beautiful creature I've ever seen. Her touches, her kisses, her scent—I can still taste her on my lips. I feel myself losing what little grip I have left on my control.

Rhianne has a way of pushing me to the brink of whatever restraint I have left. I've never met a woman as intoxicating, someone who can make me feel so much for her.

I've never been afraid of anything in my life, but Rhianne makes me feel fear. Fear of losing her, of losing myself in her.

I got so caught up in the moment that I nearly did something I swore I never would do again. At that moment, I could feel the venom start to pool in my fangs. The need to sink my teeth into her, nearly unbearable—the need to feed, overwhelming. The thought of her blood coursing through my veins is enough to send me over the edge. I can barely keep myself from going back to her now and finishing what we started.

A pang of pain radiates through my body, and my stomach clenches. I squeeze my eyes shut and double over, withering in agony. My torso wracks with dry, awful heaves. I've been so weak to my craving...

As the pangs settle, I swallow hard and realize I've been standing here, doubled over for several minutes.

My head throbs. With everything in me, I want to go back to Rhianne, to explain everything, to make her understand. I can't. I'm too hungry, and weak.

I shut off the water, dry, and dress. But, even in the hallway, I can smell her again...my senses are so attuned to her that the scent of her sex reaches me from all the way down the corridor. I want Rhianne again—more than anything I've ever wanted in my entire life. All I want to do is go back to my Amata and take her over, and over, and over. For hours even days on end. My eyes fall shut, I know that if I return to her, I'll never want to leave. I thought it was bad before, but now I feel like my blood is on fire, like I'll die if I don't taste her again. For the second night in a row, I barely manage to make it to the guest room.

I lean against the closed door for support. My whole body is shaking, my fangs are pulsing; I can feel the venom pooling in my mouth again, making it impossible to control myself. I want to taste her, to feel her against me, to be inside of her again. I've been going out of my mind all night.

I pass the dresser, rummaging over it for a paper and pen, and begin to write.

My eyes rest upon the small velvet box that I had planned to give her this evening. I take a deep breath and shove the ring into my pocket. I can't do it, not like this. I can't breathe, I can't think. All I can do right now is want, and hurt...

*I can't risk it. I can't.*

Holding on for as long as I can, I manage to stagger across the room, throw wide the window and grip the sill. Moonlight spills in from above, the cold autumn wind washes over me, I tilt my face toward the night sky and make a silent prayer to whatever greater being might be out there.

*Forgive me, Rhianne...please, don't hate me for what I must do.*

# RHIANNE

*A Few Days Later*

I sit at my desk, finding myself, once again, on the verge of tears. I feel like a fool—a blithering, helpless fool.

I re-read the letter from Sephtis for what feels like the hundredth time today, the letter he left me before he completely disappeared just a few nights ago.

*My Dearest Amata,*

*I can't stay here and see you every day, knowing what I do, and how you make me feel. I can't be near you, if I don't stop myself, I feel I will do something that I'd never be able to forgive myself for. I can only repay you for your kindness by leaving. But I beg you, when you doubt me, when you are frightened, or lonely, remember that this is my promise to you:*

*I will always love you.*

*- Sephtis.*

I swallow back the knot in my throat, and hot, angry tears burn in my eyes, I wipe them away as quickly as possible. How dare he even have the audacity to claim he loves me?

I lean back in my chair, and for a moment, I glare at the letter--a letter that tells me absolutely nothing.

What was I thinking? Things like love at first sight, and fantastical romance only happen in the movies, not in real life. I waited for him to return thinking he might have just needed some space, or time. I left the lights on for him...but he was simply gone. That night after ravishing me he just up and left. I'd taken two sick days off of work, feeling his absence like a physical illness.

*He changed. Just like that.*

I can still smell him, feel him...the imprint of his body on mine. The image of him is so vivid in my mind, that I think I'm going to go crazy.

It was over before it could even begin. I replace the note into my pocket, and stare blankly at my computer screen, still feeling the tingle of tears in my eyes.

He got what he wanted. I feel like a stupid little girl who tried to play house with a man who wanted nothing to do with her.

*Rhianne, you only knew him for a few days; you shouldn't feel this way. Rhianne, he isn't even human—you definitely shouldn't feel this way. Your first red flag should have been him telling you you're his wife on the first night you met; how'd you even fall for that one?*

I can't believe I believed him. I can't believe I fell for his lies. His sweet talk. I was so naive.

I startle when I feel a gentle hand fall on my shoulder. "Hey there, anybody home?" A voice asks behind me.

I glance up, and my face falls when I see Charlotte—I hadn't even noticed her walk in. Her brows draw tight, and she looks me over worriedly. "Rhia, what's wrong? You look like you've been crying...are you okay? It's not Todd again is it?"

"No, no—definitely not Todd." I shake my head laughing humorlessly. "Don't worry Charlotte," I dry my eyes, and force a smile. "I'm fine. I'll tell you about it later, just...not now."

"Fine, I'll wait," Charlotte says, she places her hands on her hips. "So, are you going to say it, or do I have to drag it out of you?"

"What do you mean?" My eyebrows arch up in question.

Charlotte smiles like the Cheshire cat. "Um, hello? How about that fine man, a.k.a, your husband?!"

"Will you stop yelling?" Heat rises in my cheeks, and I let my forehead drop into my hands. "His name is Sephtis, and there's nothing to tell. He's my...it's complicated."

"So he's *not* your husband?" Charlotte says casting her eyes to the ceiling. I can see her mind working as she purses her lips. "Because from what I heard, he made sure everyone knew you were his wife. Todd's still shitting himself, by the way—everyone says he kind of had it coming though. "

I chuckle. "I noticed, Todd's decided to make himself sparse instead of harassing me. In fact, he's actually been a lot more respectful."

*But Sephtis made himself even sparser.*

I bite the side of my lip for a moment, before meeting Charlotte's gaze once more. "Sephtis and I, we eloped. It happened pretty quickly, so we've been keeping it quiet so we can enjoy the peace of it. We plan to have a wedding eventually, but right now, we just want to focus on one another." The lie flies out of my mouth so fast that for a moment even I believe it.

"Ah, that makes sense why I haven't seen you wearing a ring."

"Yeah," I reply glancing down, just noticing my naked ring finger, "That's the reason."

"I totally get it. Listen, I mean, no disrespect, but the man is gorgeous. I've never seen any man pull off hair that long before. It's giving mythical creature, ancient warrior god, and that's right up my alley. All I know is that you better invite me to the wedding so one of his friends can be my wedding sex."

My jaw drops and can't help but burst out laughing. "Charlotte!"

"What, Rhia? I mean, if I had a man like that, I'd hope one or some of his friends was into me."

"No offense taken," I say, but I sober just as quickly. "Although I doubt any of his friends would interest you."

"Dammit, not one of them is good-looking?"

"I'd say more like they would eat your heart out." *And break it too.*

Charlotte furrows her brow but waves off the comment. "Anyway, that brings me to the actual reason I stopped by," Charlotte glances at the clock behind me. "Come walk with me, so I don't have to yell at you."

I rise from my seat, grab my coat and purse, and follow Charlotte for a lunch break as she walks down the hallway.

"So," Charlotte starts and then pauses. She glances back at me and then continues. "I'm not one for gossip, but I heard...they found something of Gary's..."

"W-what?"

"Same thing I said." Charlotte shook her head. "In the middle of the woods, like forty miles away, not in Mexico like they thought he was..."

"Let me guess...i-in a pit?" I offer.

"No," says Charlotte, and I blink. "There aren't any pits in those woods—as far as I know anyway. Well, they found his wallet in the middle of the woods, like forty miles away...and aside from his ID, it was completely empty."

"What do you mean?"

“I mean exactly what I said. No cash, no credit cards, nothing. Like he didn’t have a penny to his name. His friends and family swear he had enough money to last him through the rest of his life and they didn’t have a clue where it went." Charlotte shrugs. "Apparently, the guy was a multi-millionaire...I guess he left his ID behind, along with his old identity. But, just wait until you hear the rest...I heard his wallet was bloodstained. And the blood was Gary's.”

"But Gary himself..."

"They have no clue where he is. It's like he vanished off the face of this earth."

My mind is too busy reeling at the information that I hardly process half of Charlotte’s words.

# Rhianne

When I get home that evening, it's to an empty house. It isn't like I should expect anything different, but I suppose a part of me was still holding out. I stand in the foyer and take in everything. The house is clean, as always, I walk through the kitchen and living room feeling out of sorts. I even accidentally step on Mr. Muffin's tail and earn myself a swift swipe at my ankles and a hiss.

But my heart pounds as I come across a package sitting on the coffee table. It definitely hadn't been here when I'd left. It's wrapped in brown paper and tied with what looks like twine, but when I feel it, I recognize the material instantly, silk. On the front, there is a small card reading: *Rhianne*. It's Sephtis's writing. Curiously, my hand grazes the parcel's brown paper wrapping.

I take it with me to the couch and unwrap it carefully, and hold my breath as I let the paper fall away. Neat stacks of monetary notes are revealed.

"Sephtis?" I ask, redundantly.

I glance around the room and then back down at the table. Somewhere in that money is enough for anyone to live off of for a lifetime, with more to spare. I can't believe there is this much, I can only guess at where this has come from. I glance back to the front of the parcel and open the small envelope on its side, there is another note within.

*My Amata,*

*I will always provide for you, know that this money is for you and your needs. No more shall you have to endure the vices of your former boss or any man. I have left you with a small sum of money to meet your needs. If I have wronged you, then I hope my gesture might someday aid you in forgiving me. Remember, I love you.*

*Always,*

*Sephtis.*

I'm upset, this is not what I want. I don't want the occasional letter, or provision, or gift. I want *him,* I want him here, I want a life together—not this.

But the thought comes to mind just as quickly. I had called him here before, the very first night we met, he'd said I brought him to me, because we were tied to one another. He said I had that power over him. If that's true, then I can do it again. All I have to do is say his name.

*I can do this.*

I close my eyes. "Sephtis—" I say, my lips barely parting. I open them and stare hard in front as if I am expecting him to appear right at this moment. For one quick moment, I can almost feel him, his presence an overwhelming thing.

Only, nothing happens. I breathe out the breath I've been holding. The room's utter silence and emptiness mock me.

I close my eyes and picture his face, his long dark hair, his deep red eyes, sultry and filled with longing. I imagine the feel of his lips on my own, the smell of him, the warmth of him pressed against my own body.

My arms are shaking, I raise them above my head. I clasp my hands together, my fingers interlocked. Concentrating on my thoughts as hard as I can, I think of Sephtis, of his smile, his laugh, his kisses, his heartbeat against mine. I fantasize about the idea of him, what it would feel like to have him here with me.

"Sephtis..." my voice is a whisper, but I continue putting all of my emotions into my voice. "Sephtis, I need you. So please, come to me."

The world stands still. The room freezes, everything seems frozen in time. I don't see it, but I feel the air dance around my body, like a million butterfly wings. I hear a crackle in the air, as though it's filled with electricity. My breath catches in my throat, my eyesight blurs with the sting of tears as I see his shape materialize before me—

"Sephtis!"

His eyes meet mine, burning into me as he appears before me.

He reaches for me and I go for him. His touch is electric, a thousand volts of pleasure, his hands are like fire, hot to the touch, burning my skin, but in the best way possible. I meet his lips with my own and kiss him with everything I have. "Seph, the money. I don't care about the money—"

"Rhianne—"

"I just want you!"

"Rhianne..." Sephtis pulls back and touches my chin, bringing my gaze up to meet his own. "You should not have called me back."

"I had to see you," I say. "I want this, I want you."

"Rhianne, I beg of you—"

"Don't beg, Sephtis, just stay."

"Rhianne!" He pulls away from me and my eyes widen. He plants two hands on my shoulders, and cups my face in the others, holding it between his palms. "Don't you understand?" His voice is a tremulous whisper.

"Sephtis," I stop myself, and take a breath. "I want you to be with me—"

"And I love you."

The words make me pause, and I look at him in surprise, then anger. "You have a funny way of showing it."

"But it's true. I have from the moment we met." He says, but he takes a step back, his dark eyes are flashing a brighter and brighter red. He looks as if he is in pain. "But I can't be with you. It's as you said, we're not the same..."

It's only now that I realize he's changed back to his inhuman, spider-like form. He's as he was the night I met him, and yet, he is just as beautiful—no, much more so than any man.

He turns away from me, and his long hair falls before his face. "Amata, I left out of your best interest..."

"You don't want this, Sephtis. I want you, and you want me. I can see it in your eyes."

"Yes, Rhianne. I do want you. I want you too much..." His face comes closer to mine, and his words hang in the air. "I thought we could work, that I could temper my hunger and desire. Amata, I cannot be with you— what I need would destroy you."

"How do you know it wouldn't work, when you haven't even given us a fair shot?" I glare at him. "Did you feel that way when you were fucking me? Or did you decide that after the fact?"

"Don't you understand that is why? When I'm around you, my control slips; it's like you're a drug I can't resist...do you know how close I came to—" He can't bring himself to continue, instead he lets out a deep breath and pushes his hand through his hair. He drags me close and kisses me, long and slow. I feel his hunger growing as our lips move together. "I have never felt the way I do about you, not once in my life. But, I cannot do this...I cannot be with you, Rhianne. I understand that now."

His words only make my emotions boil over. "You know damn well you're the one who spouted all this stuff about me being your *Amata*, you came to my home, and my place of work and declared you were my husband. I wasn't even ready for something like marriage, but when you manage to convince me to finally give us a chance, suddenly that's when you decide we're too different? Suddenly after trying so hard to prove to me that you'd never hurt me? Well, you have hurt me! What happened to the man I fell in love with?"

Sephtis's eyes grow wide at my admission.

The words even startle me, but I continue anyway. "The man I fell in love with, that man would never fuck me and run away like a damn coward...You played me Sephtis." I accuse. I see Sephtis's handsome face fall. "And I'm no longer going to fall victim to your game."

"I never wanted to play games. I am still your husband, Rhianne," Sephtis reaches a hand out to me but I take a step back, the way his face falls then sends a painful pang through my chest.

"I don't need a husband who's barely in my life!" I snap at him, my eyes stinging. "If you love me, if you want to be with me, you'd want us to figure out how to be together—"

Sephtis says, calmly. "As your husband, we can only be together by being apart. It must be this way, I am protecting you."

"I don't need to be protected from my own decisions. I'm not a child."

"And I am not human." His voice is as sharp as his gaze.

"No kidding, Sephtis. What exactly are you?" I ask him, taking a step forward. "You owe me the truth. And this time you won't distract me with sex because I won't be falling for that again. Tell me everything I deserve to know."

"Rhianne—"

"Answer me." I take a deep breath, my heart pounding in my chest, and wait.

Sephtis exhales a deep sigh of resignation. Crossing his lower arms, and pushing the upper ones back through his forelocks, he gazes into the distance as he carefully works out where to begin.

"My species have been around for some time." He eventually says. "We precede many of the supernaturals that you read about in stories and watch in poorly depicted movies. There are many creatures in the world that you've never heard of. Some of which hide in plain sight, unseen by human eyes. I am one of them, we just are not as prideful as humans, so we don't feel the need to boast about it...no offense."

I smile wryly despite the tension in the air. "None taken. So then, where are you from?"

"My home and the name of my species have been lost in translation a long time ago. Even if I said them to you, you wouldn't understand. The closest thing would probably be Ancients, or Old Ones, and even those are not accurate. Some call us Weavers of Illusion. We long predate even many other Ancients, even those that humans regard as legendary. The Sphinx, for instance, is my kith."

"I...I thought the Sphinx was a legend."

"So did most," he says. "While there are many stories about the Sphinxes, the stories of my species are wordless ones; they go unto ld...because we don't want them told."

His words hang in the air and I can't help the shiver that runs through me at the implication.

"Amata, I must tell you what I did on the night you summoned me to you. I returned to the pit and fed on Gary. Then I manipulated footage of both him and you, weaving the illusions that my people do." he said. "I know you already guessed my hand in that, but I still need to tell you. He had suitcases of money in the trunk of his car. I took those too. Did you know he begged me to free him? Broken ribs, arms and all--he told me he'd never touch you again, that his stolen funds were insured, that he'd be a good person....if only I would let him live. His dying thoughts were so lucid to me—they're always so crystal clear when someone's about to meet their fate..."

The silence around us is more deafening than it had been before.

"And you?—" I whisper, barely able to force out the question.

My skin prickles at his response; "I told him, that is perfect—the money will make a lovely gift for my wife." He purrs out a silken reply, his eyes glinting in the half-light of the room. "I took his life, Amata, I devoured him--drained him of his blood, and innards because I was brutally hungry. It had been many, many years since I had last fed—I don't know how long. I was on the verge of death...I have a never-ending need for blood and flesh. Starved as I was, I could not stop myself. And yet, I do not wish to do that to you. I wanted to be able to live with you, and share a life with you, and yet I cannot. Even for the one I love, I cannot curb this hunger."

I hug myself and watch Sephtis, who watches me as well. "You never harmed me. But, you think we can't work?" I ask.

"I know... " he mutters somberly, "because I've tried before."

My mind is suddenly flooded with memories: the first night Sephtis had slept in the guest bedroom, how he'd suffered a nightmare, and called out in his sleep, distraught and begging forgiveness.

"You had a wife." My words are a statement, not a question.

# Sephtis

Rhianne looks up at me, her misty brown eyes are wide, dappled like the eyes of a newborn fawn, filled with confusion and uncertainty. There's a furrow in her brow.

I let my eyes fall shut and nod once. I sigh, this is not how I wanted my Amata to find out, but then again, I suppose there would never be a right time.

"You were tied to someone else? A different Amata?"

My eyes snap open, "No, that bond we did not share. Being tied to someone in that way is very rare. Very different. She was not my soulmate, but I loved her."

"I don't understand, then how did she become your wife?" Rhianne stares at me, imploring me to continue.

So I continue, my voice distant and tired: "I selected her. As king, it was a rule that I must take a wife."

"*And*, you're a king?" I see Rhianne's eyes grow wide.

"Was." I say with a small and wry smile. "I gave it up to stay here, with her....it was long ago. Long before you were born."

I hold a hand out, and Rhianne takes it, allowing me to lead her to the couch where I coax her down to sit. I crouch before her, holding hands, fingers intertwined.

Looking deep into my eyes, she squeezes my hand, transferring some of her warmth and strength to me, I feel it slowly seeping into my very bones and her fingers wrapping around my heart. I simply want to stay in this moment with her forever, entranced by those deep dark brown pools. Alas, it could not last forever. Breathing in her natural scent, I close my eyes and unlock the memories that have haunted me for countless years.

“Her name was Jaarah...." I pause, her name was a difficult one to speak. The sound of it makes me hurt.

I take a breath and continue, "Rhianne, my kind exists between the veils of this dimension and the next. In one of my visits here, in those very woods I met you, I saw her, heading back to her village, and I was completely enamored by her beauty. In my youth, I was so blinded by my desire for her that I couldn't see the destruction I was unleashing.”

"You were young and in love." Rhianne reasons.

"I was selfish, Amata. I made it my mission to find out who she was. When I did, I introduced myself, negating that I wasn’t human. Before long, we were involved. She didn't know the truth, that I was different, that I was a monster. At first, I did well to keep my two worlds very separate. I felt I must hide my nature because she would not have understood. She would have only been frightened of me and my people. I realize now that it was my first mistake, I was dishonest, but I was worried about how she would take it. It was incredibly selfish of me.

When she first grew suspicious of what I might be, I was unnerved--I managed to redirect her questions well enough. I tried to hide the truth for as long as I was able. I kept my visits frequent enough to keep up my lie and to pacify her. I would come to her village on the eve of some of their festivals and disguise myself among her villagers. I would stay and watch them, listening to their songs and reveling in the joy I was allowed to share with her. We'd wanted to live life and find our own happiness, eventually, I asked her to marry me."

Rhianne hangs on every word, "So what happened?" she says.

"She accepted. But to become my wife, I had to tell her *something* of what I was —though I never showed her, for fear she would reject me. I hurt her because I'd been untruthful, but still, she forgave me. There is a ceremony that my kind must partake in that would bind us since destiny did not. That is the way of my kind. The thing is, to marry in my species means to give your free will to your spouse. So, though we weren't tied through fate, we were bound by magic. If she wished it, I had to obey, and ultimately, she unwittingly used it against us both..."

"I don't understand. Why would she use that against you?"

"It wasn't her fault; in her own way, she was doing what was right. She only meant to be kind, Amata." I say, a sad smile on my face, my hand never leaving hers. I watch Rhianne's face and see the confusion there.

Feeling my tenseness, she rubs my knuckles and waits for me to relax. "This is a safe space. Whatever you want to tell me, I want to hear."

"I know," I say, grateful. "In the back of my mind, I had plans to eventually ease her into my truth—even ask her to live with me in the realm of my people as my queen...but the longer I stayed with her, the more I knew I couldn't ask her to abandon her own, the more I realized how self-centered and cruel that would be.

So, I decided to live with her instead. I would leave the village often to hunt, and that worked just as well since I could provide any game I managed to snare for what became our village, our home. But for myself, I required human quarry. I fed on outsiders...those that would mean her village harm but denied myself that prey when I was in her village. Her people became mine too.

One night, I came upon a young woman being attacked by vagrants on her way home—a friend of Jaarah's. I felt the overwhelming need to protect her, and I did. No one could have stopped me. I tore out the throats of the men who dared to harm her. But in doing so, my disguise unraveled, and she saw me for what I was.

She was already frightened by what she'd seen, and the carnage, so she was afraid of me. Before I could explain myself, she ran back to tell her village about what I truly was. But that wasn't my concern—my concern was that the village might turn on Jaarah, which is exactly what they did."

I pause. I've never told this to anyone, but I feel compelled to tell Rhianne everything.

"What? How could they?" Rhianne's grip has softened on my hand and I can still see the uncertainty and pain in her eyes.

"They were afraid of what I was. They decided that I, nor she could be trusted. I frightened them, so I wasn't upset on my own behalf, but what they did to Jaarah was unforgivable. They accused her of luring me in, of wishing to take advantage of my powers. They said she was a witch, and that I was her consort. They condemned her.

The villagers did to her what they'd wanted to do to me. They set our house on fire. They drove her from our home for taking up with a monster. They wanted to execute her. I managed to save Jaarah and flee, but she was never the same after that. She was understandably hurt and so upset that, once again, I had been dishonest with her. She demanded I reveal myself then...so I obeyed."

"What did she do?"

"She screamed. She was terrified of me. She called me a monstrosity." I laugh bitterly. "She didn't lie, and I couldn't blame her. I saw the fear in her eyes, and it made me realize I had been so wrong to keep the truth from her. She could barely look at me. She wouldn't let me touch her again... I gave her her space, holding out hope that one day, far in the future, she might come around."

"She didn't love you?" Rhianne says, her voice heavy with sorrow.

"She loved me, Rhianne, I am certain of that. And I loved her deeply. Still, the fear and anguish she felt when she looked upon me were so clear to me. That was...painful. More than that, I could feel her sorrow for all she'd lost because of me. I told her she could live amongst my kind, I could take her as my queen, and she would not have to live under judgment or scrutiny. But she longed to live among her own kind, she said she didn't want to live a life surrounded by monsters.

We finally settled on terms of living together, and we took our place in those woods. She ordered me to stay in my true form even if it repulsed her. She told me she didn't want to fall for my illusions again. I don't fault her, I was the one who had been dishonest--but it pained me to see her flinch when I'd reach out to her, when I'd give her the fish I'd caught in a stream, or fruits and nuts I scavenged from around the forest. I should have been happy that she still kept me around, but perhaps it was because she had no one else.

I had built a home for us, far from any human settlements. I left to hunt when I needed to, and provided for her in the way I knew ho w...but she grew increasingly distant and unhappy, despite my efforts. Jaarah mourned the loss of her village and people...I couldn't fulfill her happiness.

Eventually, I asked her if she wished for me to give her wide breadth, to stay outside, if it would make her more comfortable. She refused, but she told me one thing would make her happy. Eager to please and return her happiness to her, I listened. She said she'd thought about it for a long while and wanted that I should never hunt again, all in hopes that we could return to her village. Jaarah wanted to prove herself to be a pure woman and to have me prove I was a man of my word who was different than the monster they'd once thought me.

My heart broke for her then. That was the only family she ever knew, the only friends, the only human connections she had, it only made sense that she'd want to return. Deep inside, I knew that it would never work, her life as a villager was over...but, I had to obey. I promised her I wouldn't hunt, and kept my word. We made preparations for our return and talking about it excited her. Slowly, I saw the hope returning to her eyes, the smile that had left her for so long came back. I couldn't help but indulge her, perhaps I shouldn't have, but it was the only thing maintaining her will to go on. For a while, I might have even fooled myself into thinking, somehow, her plan might work. But in the meantime, I allowed myself to grow hungry and weak...I wasn't being honest about my nature, my...needs. I tried as best I could to hide my condition, but I grew sicker by the day. I was slowly dying, and it didn't take long for Jaarah to notice.

When she asked me what I needed, I told her simply enough: Living human blood. I begged her to rethink her request, I didn't want to build up her dreams and crush them, but I needed to tell her the truth, that her plan wouldn't turn out the way she hoped; Jaarah was adamant. If I could prove to her, to her village, that I could be like them, they would welcome us back with open arms." I draw in a shuddering inhale, and hold Rhianne's gaze. "But, the way her people had looked at us on the day of our exile.... I knew deep down that Jaarah's wish coming true was an impossibility. As sure as I knew I needed to hunt...else I'd lose what little control I had left, or perish."

I can't stop now. Rhianne needs to know. I need to purge myself of my guilt and shame, lay myself bare before her. I take a breath and go on. "She didn't want me to hunt, and she didn't want me starving and in pain..."

"What did she do?" Rhianne asks with bated breath, she looks so innocent, I can barely form the words that come next...

"She offered herself instead. I told her she didn't understand what I was, she didn't understand what she was asking of me, and she said that she loved me. I told her that I'd hurt her, she said she was strong enough to bear my burdens. She said: *'Take all you need from me, that is my command...'*" Tears fill my eyes as I think back to that fateful night.

"She killed herself?" Rhianne blurts, horrified her eyes wet and shining.

"No, Amata, I did." I whisper, speaking so low I fear she may not have heard me. I swallow, my throat is dry and sore, I feel bile in the back of my throat, but I force myself to continue, nearly gasping for breath. "I had no choice—I obeyed...my free will was gone, there was only hunger. I could not stop, and she could not escape. I hated myself, but I couldn't stop. Her alluring scent filled the air, I had held her to me, I had her in my arms, and my mouth on hers, and I was too weak to fight against what the magic had compelled me to do. I should have fought harder to resist, but I let my actions be guided instead." I nearly choke on my next words, feeling my insides heave. "I had kissed her on the neck, and it was the scent of her blood, the feel of her warmth, and her womanhood that filled my senses. I devoured her—and I couldn't hold myself back...Rhianne, I'm sorry—I'm sorry—I'm sorry—" I whisper over and over. Tears stream down my cheeks as I recount the story of how Jaarah died in my arms, a broken and empty shell of the vibrant woman I'd fallen in love with. "I had given up all my free will to her. I would have done anything she had asked of me. I would have done anything to protect her—instead, I was the cause of her demise. I stole her life from her and then I killed her."

I can't stop now. I need to be honest with Rhianne. "I did not mean to, but I did. The bond of magic was torn, and I was released, but it was too late. She was gone...in the end, I was heartbroken. I've been haunted by that moment ever since..."

I almost wish I hadn't said it aloud, but it was done. I can't take it back anymore. I stare at her, waiting for her to speak, to protest, to deny it. To tell me it isn't true.

Rhianne reaches out slowly, as if she's afraid she'll frighten me away. I sit motionless, willing myself to let her touch me. I've let her get too close, but I know I can't stop her any more than I could stop the dawn that day...and I want her too much to say a word. She slips her tiny hand inside mine and I hold it tight. "You didn't mean to." Rhianne's voice is soft, quivering.

"I know, but I still did it. I destroyed everything we'd built, and I broke my promise to her. I am truly monstrous. That is the way of my kind, Amata."

"No, it isn't. You had been starved. You couldn't have known. That can't be the end...what happened after that?" She insists, and my heart stirs with hope, but I know better—I know how flawed my logic is.

"After? I couldn't accept what I'd done..." I rack my weary mind to dredge up more memories, "I blamed the villagers for her death for rejecting her, for exiling her, even though she'd done nothing wrong. I decided that if she was not their people, nor was I. So I made my grand return to her village, but not to live among them. I wanted them to beg for mercy, to beg forgiveness, and beg for their lives when I stood before them. I wanted her village to know what it felt like to lose everything they loved. Like Jaarah did. Like I had. I hunted and relished in it and I killed mercilessly. The only ones who escaped were those I allowed to. I killed to feel alive because it was the only way I could feel. I felt nothing more than rage, pain, and bloodlust. I was a monster in the truest sense of the word. I no longer attempted to hide what I truly was. I was the monster in the woods."

Rhianne is quiet, I want to look at her but I'm afraid. I'm afraid of what I'll see. I'm afraid of what she may think of me.

"I have done truly terrible things, but in the end, it left me empty, because I knew even if her villagers exiled her, it was I who caused her death most of all. Had I never been in Jaarah's life, she would have lived to marry within her own kind, have children...live to old age. It was my second mistake, and after a time of consuming enough pain and misery, I no longer recognized myself. I could not repent; what I did is unforgivable—I could not even return to my own people. I was far too ashamed of what I'd done. I decided to build a grave for all those I'd killed, to give them proper burials, and finally, to live away from both worlds...and die in that pit—between your world and mine."

Rhianne's eyes are wide with terror, and then the tears fall. She flings her arms around me and buries her face into my chest. The gesture is so surprising to me that I stiffen completely.

"I wish I could say I understand exactly how you feel, Sephtis...but I really can't. I'm sorry that you suffered so much, that you experienced so much anguish that would bring you to the point of breaking—but...what I mostly feel is relief, that you are still here. I'm sorry you felt you were unforgivable, unlovable, that you felt you had to hide from the world and condemn yourself to a lone sentence of damnation—but I'm glad that you opened up to me, and that you are still here now...after all, if it weren't for you, I wouldn't be alive today."

I gaze into her eyes, and they speak of what I am only recently beginning to recognize in myself. "I heard your cries for help, Rhianne, and that was what roused something in me other than the pain I'd been wallowing in for so long. They seared into my heart, and galvanized me into action. I was on death's door that night, resigned to close my eyes and never wake again, but I heard your voice. I didn't know what Gary did to you or why I cared so deeply, but I wanted to get rid of whoever hurt you...I thought that I might be able to do one good thing before I passed away. In the end, it was you who saved me, Amata." I breathe, my eyes widening as realization hits. "That night I wanted yougone fro m that pit so that the strong feelings you evoked in me would leave wit h you, but everything in me wished I could beg you to take me wit h you. That's why I stayed silent, when you said you were sorry that I was alone because I saw no point in wishing for what could not be . When I appeared here, and realized I was tied to you, it didn't phase m e because you are perfect. You were kind to me, you knew what I was, an d you still accepted me, even grew to love me. But, I had not yet learne d my third mistake..." My hand comes up to cup the delicate curve o f her cheek, and I feel a rush of adrenaline as my mind races.

"What was that then?"

"Loving you." I whisper. Rhianne stares at me with wide eyes, as I continue, "The first time we were intimate, I was absolutely overwhelmed by your very being, your scent, the taste of you—more than any other. You are so beautiful inside and out, Rhianne. When you said: I can take all I want from you, it all felt so...karmic. I felt I would lose you...worse, that I would *take* everything from you...I am not what you think I am, Rhianne. I am not a good person. I am a monster—which is why I cannot stay with you."

She doesn't look down, but she doesn't look at me either. I can't read her expression, her emotions are guarded by a look of complete neutrality. Her fingers are tight around my hand, but she doesn't squeeze. She doesn't speak, and then she slowly, ever so slowly moves my hand to her lips and presses a gentle kiss to my palm. Her eyes meet mine, clear and serious. She looks at me like I'm the only person in the world. Her hands begin to tremble but only slightly as she reaches out and touches my face. My breath hitches at the gentle touch.

"To me, you've been the sweetest, kindest, most thoughtful man I've ever met. You protected me, you saved me when I couldn't rely on anyone else. Others might see you vastly differently Sephtis, but how can *I* ever consider you a monster?" She smiles at me, she actually smiles...I don't know how that is possible, but it's there, very real and sincere.

Again, I'm helpless as she holds my very heart in her hands.

# Rhianne

I look at him, sitting there, his face shrouded in shadows, and I feel my breath catch in my throat. I can't begin to imagine how he must feel, to be reliving such horrific events in his mind day after day, and night after night. He may have physically left the hell of his own design, but its memory is never far from his thoughts. I have to do something...I have to help him break through.

"What happened between Jaarah and you was a mistake, one with a heavy toll...but, you both loved each other. What had happened was neither of your faults." I whisper, waiting for him to look at me as I say it, so he can hear me in my truest intent. "She died for you, the person she loved most, her love for you was greater than her fear... and yet, she wasn't the only one who paid a price that day." I reach out, taking his hand.

He looks up at me, his eyes searching mine.

"You have to forgive yourself because you're no longer the same person. You don't have to keep punishing yourself or be alone anymore. I know you, and I know that you wouldn't do anything to hurt me..." I smile at him, squeezing his hand. I see the tears rolling down his cheeks, and I wipe them away.

"Meeting you was the first time I ever wanted to live for something ever since...and I'm so glad I did." His eyes meet mine then, and I soak in the hope I see in them.

“I'm glad you did too, I'm so grateful to have met you.” My heart pounds furiously in my chest, a very real and physical thing and we fall together into a kiss. I feel it pulling me into itself, and I am nearly helpless to resist but I manage to pull back. “I am only with you, so I hope you want to be with me too.” I stare at him, searching his face, waiting for his reaction.

His eyes close, as if he’s letting out a breath he’d been holding, his lips part, and he whispers. “Do you really mean that?”

I shrug. “I might be a little crazy, but I think I do mean it,” I say smiling playfully. “Besides, you would be a terrible husband if you didn’t, and Mr. Muffins would miss you too much.”

He draws me in with all four arms into a tight embrace, burying his face in my neck, crushing me against him, and I feel his body shaking in relief. He presses his lips against mine. His hands are in my hair, his body is pressed against mine, and I want him inside me more than I’ve wanted anything in my life.

“I won't run from you...and I'm yours...but only if you are mine too. Sephtis, stay with me, in my world, and in yours. Be mine.”

“I already am yours, Rhianne...” He replies, and his eyes flash with a fiery light.

I shiver as he slips a hand under my shirt and runs his fingers down my spine, a sweet ache rises in my belly.

“I mean it. I’m not giving you up again. You’ve already broken my heart once, I’ll have you know that I won’t take it lightly next time.”

I reach out and spread my fingers against him, trying to capture the warmth and feel of him. I want to keep him here, with me, like this.

"Command it of me, Amata." His lips brush against mine. "I am yours to have and to hold, my heart is yours for eternity."

He kisses me again and I pull away, giggling at his persistence. I'm laughing, and he's holding me against him, his mouth on mine. "I'm so glad you came back." I moan into his lips.

He pulls me onto his lap, and despite the differences in our anatomy, I fit perfectly in his embrace. I settle comfortably, feeling warm and safe and oh, so incredibly aroused. He presses his face into my hair, inhaling my scent. "Me too. I don't ever want to be without you..." His voice is hoarse with need. "You are my beacon in the darkness, Rhianne." He says, lowering his head to my neck, his breath hot against my skin.

I gasp, my eyes fluttering closed as his hands move up my shirt. He moves slow and gently, his lips brushing against my neck and my collarbone.

"I'm not planning on going anywhere." Sephtis breathes into me.

"You don't have a choice." I say, I feel a rush of happiness as he nips me gently. I lose my breath and moan.

He pulls back and looks at me with a gleam in his eyes I've never seen before. He presses his lips against mine again and I can feel his fangs on them, but I don't care. I want this, I want him. I want us.

"It seems we should take this upstairs." He says, moving to put me down.

"No—" I protest with a labored breath. "I don't want to go upstairs, I don't want you to transform, I want you as you are, just like this."

I let out a delightful squeal as he suddenly lifts me up, his four arms helping him to carry me effortlessly.

He smirks and runs his hands over my body. "Even like this?"

“You're beautiful like this, so beautiful, Sephtis," My fingers tips brush against his face gently.

He blinks, his eyes darkening yet brighter than ever, his pupils widening, “You are beautiful, Rhianne. You are exquisite. I’ve never seen anything like you in my life. I want to worship you like this. I want to cover every inch of your body with my tongue, and with my hands, with my silk...I want to have you in every way possible, and feel you come undone in my arms...”

“Please.” I breathe, my voice so sweet and soft he could mistake it for a whisper, but his hands are already removing my top, leaving me in just my bra. Pulling the cups down, he leans in and takes one of my nipples in his mouth, sucking hard and biting it gently. “Sephtis...” I let my head fall back, moaning, “You’re making me crazy, please.” The blood rushes to my already inflamed clit, making me squirm in his hold.

Gripping my buttocks in both lower hands, he moves the others to the button of my pants, pulling it open.

"Yes," I whisper, as he moves his thumb to my clit, teasing me into a wonderful frenzy. I feel frustrated and lust-filled. "I want you, Sephtis."

Just as quickly, he drags my pants off of me, tossing them to the ground with my discarded blouse. Now he grips two handfuls of my ass and spreads my slick folds with his thumbs. Sephtis leans forward, to lave and tease my clit beneath its hood, before sucking it hard, his tongue twisting and swirling around it mercilessly. He gazes deep into my eyes as he runs his tongue along my wet slit, from my clit all the way to my asshole, and back again.

I spread my legs for him, gasping for air.

His red gaze never leaves my face as his tongue ravages me, teasing and exploring every inch of my pussy with tongue and teeth.

It's too intense, I break eye contact as they roll back in ecstasy.

And then I feel him slip a finger inside me, exploring my tight wet heat. “I love you, Rhianne...” His words are a purr against my lips as he thrusts his finger in and out of me, building the intensity until I'm panting with need.

I clench around him, reveling in the sensations. I want to respond to him, but his mouth is back on me again, sucking my clit, feasting until I'm calling out his name in a high-pitched moan. Tears sting my eyes, but he only pulls me closer.

One of his hands slides up to my throat, squeezing just enough to make my juices flow harder.

My fingers dig into his broad shoulders for dear life, and I grind my hips against him in earnest.

He pushes another finger inside me, my pussy stretching to accommodate him as he moves his fingers in a come-hither motion. And his tongue never lets up, only moving faster and rougher, nipping and sucking at my clit until I'm a writhing mess in his arms.

I can't help but cry out as an explosive orgasm rips through me from the expert stroking of his tongue and fingers.

He keeps up the same relentless pace until I can no longer take it, until I'm beyond satisfied. It's too much... I come again, a warm fountain flowing over his hand.

He takes a break from licking and sucking me long enough to draw his fingers out of me slowly, bring them to his lips, and suck them clean with a low groan that's pure sin. The sight of his tongue lapping at my own juices is so erotic, but his eyes gleam with the promise of more.

I'm still hovering in the clouds when he slips his fingers back in, nearly stirring them within me, while peppering a rain of warm kisses along each of my thighs before finally rising up to meet my face again, our mouths interlocking in a kiss as sweet as it is passionate. The feel of his warm tongue slipping into my mouth, wet with my own taste is a heady sensation. Our tongues tangle into one another, as we share the same breath.

I break the kiss only to gasp. "I love you, Sephtis...I always will." I pull his face to mine and kiss him again. I can feel my own wetness against him, and I am ready to take him.

He leans in and bites me on the neck. His teeth are a sharp contrast to the gentle kisses he showered me with moments before. His lips press against my throat as his teeth sink in, a sensation that sends a sharp thrill up my spine. And then I feel the slow release of his intoxicating, addictive elixir like a gentle stream as his fangs slide deeper into my neck. The sensation comes with an intense rush, a soothing warmth that radiates through my veins and deep into my core. It spreads throughout my body like fire, an intense pleasure that takes me to the edge and keeps pushing me further. I'm lost in a sea of ecstasy, and the only thing tethering me back to reality is his touch.

"Come for me, Amata." He moans against my ear and I do almost instantly.

My whole body shakes and I cling to him, every nerve-ending alight with pleasure. My whole body is alive, my inner muscles clenching down, trying to milk his fingers. My moans get louder and louder, as I writhe against them.

With his fingers still inside of me, he moves his thumb to my clit and rubs it in slow circles, and again, I come apart at the seams with a scream. He moans against my neck, easing his mouth over my throat and his tongue is a velvet caress against my skin, leaving behind a tingling sensation.

My whole body is vibrating with a desire that only grows, the climax still rippling through me.

With one spider-like appendage, he pulls silk from his spinnerets; it stretches before me like a silvery ribbon. He takes my wrists in his hands and ties them together with the silken cord, binding them securely in gentle but firm circles. I moan at the feeling of being restrained, of his silk slipping softly, sensually along my flesh, around my breasts, my waist, and my thighs, mapping my body while sweetly eliciting my yielding. He works faster than I can keep track of, my mind racing with excitement and anticipation. I close my eyes, breathless, and throbbing with desire. I feel him wrap the silk around my hips, a gentle pull bringing me closer.

“Keep your eyes on me, Amata." His voice is a low and growling purr, and my eyes meet his. Then as soft as a whisper, he says: “You're doing such a good job.”

The silk creates intricate patterns as it winds its way around my curves and traverses the planes of my body, tightening securely with each knot Sephtis makes.

I test a tug back against the restraints, and he gives me a knowing smile. He slowly tightens the knots on the silken cords around me, but carefully avoids cutting off circulation.

This is what I want; this is what I crave. Thoroughly immobilized, I know I am at his mercy, and I have never felt so safe in my life.

Sephtis pulls the silk loincloth from around his waist, I watch as the incredible length of his erection emerges from behind the obsidian-colored chitinous plates at his groin, his cock beaded with dew and curved toward his stomach, the thick head sitting atop a thick stalk of flesh, glistening and wet. He moves closer, the hard carapace of his lower body pressing against my softer flesh.

I can feel the silken cords biting into my wrists, and tightening around my whole body as he uses them to draw me closer.

His cock rubs against my clit, sending shocks of pleasure through me.

I moan and writhe against him.

Sephtis lifts me higher, moving me away from his cock and I whimper in protest. He chuckles softly and runs the head of his dick along my slick, swollen folds, teasing me.

I arch my back and thrust my hips toward him, silently begging him to enter me.

He lifts me high over his shaft, as he looks intently into my eyes.

My position is restrained, graceful, and vulnerable. I am forced to just hang there, desperate to feel him pound into me.

"Beg me, Amata." He demands. He holds me over him, just out of reach, and I feel him rubbing the glistening head of his cock against my swollen lips.

I cry out in frustration and twist against my bonds. "Please, please!"

The heat of his shaft against my opening is too much to bear. He lets me down, but not quickly enough. I wish I had more words, but my lust is making it hard to think. I squirm against him and pull against the silken cords. The tightness makes me ache further. How can I possibly feel more desperate than this? "Seph—" I whimper.

Finally, he obliges.

In a fluid movement that is shocking to both of us, he lowers my body so I slide down his long, thick cock, and I can't help my arched back and shriek of bliss as he fills me inch by glorious inch, stretching me so incredibly wide.

My mind spirals into a place of pure pleasure where only he exists. My back arches further, and I can feel him sinking even deeper into me. I find myself lifted up again and allowed to slide down again, harder this time until my ass is pressed firmly against his groin.

He grunts, loudly and deeply, the muscles of his shoulder and arm rippling as he lifts me up and lets me plunge down onto him again.

The shock of him filling me every time I swallow him makes my head spin.

Still suspending me in the air, he grips my hips with two hands, moving me up and down his straining shaft at a sensual pace that almost drives me crazy.

I cry out as he starts to roll his hips in a slow, steady rhythm, taking his time, the sound of my voice bouncing off the walls and echoing around us.

Sephtis's cock throbs inside of me and I can feel him pull out slowly, leaving a hot trail behind and making me whimper with need. He thrusts back in, faster, harder, and says my name in a strangled moan, his cock pulsing against me, our bodies slapping together in a frantic rhythm. He holds me close as he pounds into me, our hearts beating as one. As he continues, faster and harder, he sucks and nips at each of my swollen nipples. The sensations radiating from them each time send bursts of pleasure throughout my whole body.

I moan in wild abandonment, consumed by the waves of utter pleasure that course through me. I feel my walls clench around him and I know I am ready to come again. The pleasure is intense, building until it explodes within me and I am screaming Sephtis's name.

He gives one final thrust, the silken cords digging into my flesh pulling me hard against him and I shatter into a million pieces.

My legs violently shake, and Sephtis breathes into my ear. "Enjoy it, Amata," he says, as my muscles convulse around him again and his jaw flexes. "Your orgasms are addictive, and you look so beautiful when you come."

His thrusts hit my sweet spot again, and I feel yet another orgasm, building in the pit of my stomach. "Sephtis, I love you—"

The string of words is cut off as another climax hits me and I scream as I fall apart again, my voice bouncing off the walls. I feel his cock grow as if he is trying to get even deeper inside me.

"I love you so much," he whispers, as he slows his thrusts.

I look up at him, tears forming in my eyes.

He nods. "I do. I love you with everything in me." Increasing his intensity, Sephtis connects our lips in a deep kiss. He growls and I feel every muscle in his body tighten, every tendon, every sinew flexing as he finds his release.

My core is throbbing and pulsing, and he fills me to the brim with hot ropes of his seed spilling over my trembling muscles, holding my gaze as he empties himself into me. The sensation of his cum filling my pussy is almost too much, and I cry out.

He lets out a little grunt, and I feel my insides shudder and shake. My mind goes blank.

He closes his eyes, his breathing is labored, and he doesn't move for a moment, his forehead resting on my shoulder. Then, slowly he unlaces the silk bondage from around my body and pulls the rest of it out of the way. His cock slides out of me, and I feel a little dizzy, my entirety still shaking with the aftershocks of our lovemaking. He catches me before I fall, his arms like steel as he holds me in place, and then pulls me into a hug. Cradling my head against his shoulder, he says, "I love you, and I will never stop."

My heart melts, and I can't hold back the wave of emotion that washes over me. Tears stream from my eyes, and I throw my arms around him, pulling him close. I can't form words; I don't even know what I'm feeling, but I'm sure that I've never been so happy in my life. "I love you too," I whisper, "And I'll never stop loving you."

Sephtis glances down at the red lines of beauty left on my flesh from his bondage and brushes his lips along them, his kiss both gentle and tender; he takes my breath away with its sweetness. I close my eyes, feeling so cherished and loved at that moment as if nothing else matters apart from us being together like this.

We stay like that for what seems like an eternity until finally, Sephtis slowly disengages from our embrace and I open my eyes. Raising his head, his dark gaze holds mine before he kisses my lips gently, "I have something important to ask you."

I look at him, his face is solemnly serious. I nod, "You know you can ask me anything."

"Rhianne, I know I'm a monstrous thing—" I stop his words and kiss him passionately.

Releasing him, I look him deeply in the eyes. "You are not a monstrous thing. Do you hear me?" I caress the side of his face. "You are the most amazing man I've ever met in my life. Tell me what you'd like to ask."

"Well, the wedding cake cooking show I watched made me realize I missed a very important step in your culture." He raises a closed fist before me. "I bought this on the day of our dinner date. I was going to ask you after dinner, but, we ended up in bed instead..."

"You bought what?" I ask, my eyes widening.

Sephtis tilts his head to one side and arches a brow. "You really don't know?"

"It just seems too good to be true." I shake my head. "I don't believe it."

"Believe it, Amata. I want to ask you to make me the happiest man alive and officially marry me."My eyes grow ten times their size as he unfurls his fingers and presents me with a small velvet box, seemingly out of nowhere. Opening it, the diamond inside seems to make the entire room brighter.

Tears spill down my cheeks as he takes the ring from the box, placing it on the tip of my finger; he looks at me. "You saved me in more ways than I could ever thank you for, and I want to spend the future years showing you how grateful I am for you. I'm not sure what those days will look like, or how the years to come will come to be, but what I know is that I want to spend them with you. Will you marry me?"

Nodding frantically, I slide my finger through the ring. "Yes! One thousand times yes!" I cry and wrap my arms and legs around him.

"Thank you, thank you, Amata. I'm so happy to hear that," he whispers. And now that he's bound me, there's nothing else he wants more than to take me over and over again. And he does, sinking his fangs deep into my flesh, his four hands roving all over my body as we writhe together in ecstasy, our cries of pleasure echoing throughout the room. Passion overtakes us both, and we become lost in each other's arms, consumed by throbbing desire. For hours on end, we lose ourselves in a whirlwind of passion that leaves us utterly sated and content.

My heart pounds with love for this magnificent creature that has completely entwined himself around my body - my soul - forever.

# Rhianne

Our fervent lovemaking leaves me so sore in all the right places, Sephtis's rare combination of fierce passion, strength, and tenderness is more than I ever imagined. My body is stretched, marked by him, and the recovery is slow but rewarding. I'm grateful that he devotes this time to simply embracing me, his fingers tracing languidly along the curves of my body. I'm so elated to have him back, that I can't help but smile like an idiot when we're snuggled up, reclining on the couch together. He smiles back at me, and we simply hold each other as the night passes by, Mr. Muffins curled up and dozing contentedly by our feet.

Sephtis has regained his human form, much more fitting for our house in his opinion, though I don't think I care either way—in some ways, I've started to prefer his true form.

The television is on and tuned into the late-night news. I feel Sephtis's arms tight around me, both of us looking at the screen. It's all boring, local news.

I can tell that Sephtis is in a better mood, so I finally get the nerve to ask him about the past few days.

Turning to him, I start up, "Where did you go? When you were away the past while?"

He is silent for a moment before he answers. "I attempted to hun t...to feed. For a short, while, I pursued a man stumbling around...d runk." he says softly.

"What happened?"

He takes a deep breath in and releases it. "I couldn't. In the end, I let him escape. It was tough, Rhianne, I gave up the chase, I let him go."

I know that he's talking about his urges, his need for blood. It's not getting any better for him, and he's trying to stay strong against it.

"But you're going to have to feed at some point..." I say, looking at him sadly. "Or you'll starve, like before."

"I know." He puts his hand on top of mine. His gaze is fixed on the television now, as I stare intently at him. "But I know what I'll do if I ever feel you might be in danger from me, Amata."

His gaze settles upon mine.

"That's not a solution," I say, knowing exactly what he's thinking.

"If ever I feel my urges are growing too strong, I have resigned myself to my fate, Amata. Know that I will never allow myself to harm you. It's the only way..." He pulls me tight against himself.

I'm no longer paying attention to the news, but Sephtis is. His eyes suddenly narrow, and he grasps my hand tightly. I look at the TV. The talking head on the news is speaking about reports of a man, wanted for multiple counts of rape and battery, and suspected murder. He was still on the run. Suddenly my heart is beating loudly in my chest, as I stare at the screen.

"It's him..." Sephtis says, his voice low, barely a whisper.

Realization dawns on me, "The man you let escape?" I glare at the screen. My horrific experience with Gary suddenly arises in the surface of my mind. How helpless he made me feel, I feel myself tremble with anger.

"Yes." His jaw tightens, I can see the muscles flex as he grits his teeth together.

I run my hand up his chest. "Maybe there is a way you can sustain yourself without hurting innocent people...and a way to redeem yourself in the eyes of human beings."

Sephtis turns to me.

"You can become a protector, hunt the people who deserve to be hunted. People who fancy themselves predators and hurt people more vulnerable than they are." I say, my gaze still focused on the criminal pictured on the screen.

"Tell me, Rhianne...what would you have me do?" He says.

"Make the world a better, safer place," I reply. "And make the world a nightmare for people who make the world unsafe for others."

"And hunt him?" he asks, his hand caressing my hair.

I nod my head before placing a gentle kiss on top of his muscular chest.

"Yes, because you're a good man, Sephtis," I say, drawing his gaze back to me, my voice barely above a whisper. I bite the side of my lip and stroke his manhood, maintaining eye contact. He groans, his eyes reddening.

"Jaarah might have been uncomfortable being called a witch, but I'd like to think a witch can use her powers to bless as well as to curse. Can you find him?" I ask, looking up at Sephtis beneath my eyelashes.

"That would be very easy, Amata." He rumbles, and his eyes glow brightly now.

I lick my lips and lean forward, placing a gentle bite on his chest. "Then I command you, go hunt, Sephtis. And when you're finished, come back and celebrate new beginnings with your Amata."

# About Author

Lexi Esme is a writer of steamy erotic romance stories featuring beautiful black heroines of every variety and the gorgeous men (and supernatural beings) who love them. Lexis believes that everyone should be able to see themselves wined, dined, seduced, romanced, and even ravaged in their choice of romantic literature and love interests of every variety to cherish them. Seeing a lack of the kind of main love interests that look like her, she set out to create as many of these stories as she possibly can for readers who might feel the way she does or simply just want to see something new. Variety is the spice of life, after all, and Lexis loves to keep it spicy.

Based in Canada, she spends her days walking the nearby nature trails dreaming up romantic and sexy new adventures and scenarios, the steamier, the better. She also loves experimenting in the kitchen, dancing, drawing, and reading. She never ever has enough books, shoes, or chocolate.

She is currently hard at work on a new series of sexy novellas and various other erotic short stories.

Follow Lexi Esme on her socials and get updates on upcoming projects and more!

Linktree: https://linktr.ee/Lexiesme

Tiktok: @lexiesme

Instagram: @lexieesmebooks

Be on the lookout for Lexis's website!

# THANK YOU FOR READING

Thank you so much for taking the time to read this novella!

As a new writer, I'm extremely grateful that you, the reader, have even given this book a chance!

I would really, truly appreciate it if you would leave a review on Amazon, (whether you liked the book or not), it really helps me to see what my readers like and what they don't like, and I'm always striving to do better for y'all. :)

Sincerely,

Lexi Esme

# Also By Lexi Esme

**Chapter 1**

"Did you make a purchase from the lingerie store yesterday?"

The question is almost stupid. I already had the bank statement in hand but perhaps I wish he would at least have the decency to come clean with it or to tell me something that would make all of this better. Something or anything that would make it so that I didn't just waste all this time for nothing.

Jerome, the man I've wasted a year of my life on sits on my beat-up couch, laid back with his feet outstretched on the coffee table beside the X-Box I'd bought him for Christmas last year–each day I regret buying it for him more and more.

And now, my eyes settle on the couch beneath him, when I bought it, it was cream white, now it's nothing but a shade of mustard yellow from all the stains. I tried to have it deep cleaned, but it always ends up turning back into a mess so I gave up. Now, I'm starting to understand that it wasn't cleaning all the messes that I should have given up on.

I should have given up on him.

"What the hell are you talking about?" He grunts, eyes not even leaving the videogame on the TV screen as he takes a drag from his blunt and a sip from his beer.

"I'm talking about the call I just got from the bank that all of my goddamn money is gone. Purchases on beer, lingerie, and a lot of cash withdrawals that don't make any sense to me" I toss the bank statement in his direction.

"If you're going to buy your whores gifts at least don't use my fucking money!"

Now that seems to grab his attention.

He places the bottle of beer on the coffee table as he turns to face me. The look of anger on his face used to scare the living daylights out of me but now I feel nothing but remorse.

"YOUR goddamn money? Last time I checked, it's a joint account meaning whatever is in there is mine too."

"You're right. It is a joint account but the last time I *also* checked I'm the only one in this house that's been putting money in it. I mean when was the last time you even got up from that couch?" I ask, already knowing what he would answer back so I beat him to it.

"-And no, playing basketball with your friends doesn't count because you shouldn't even be hanging out with them! Not when you're barely getting by. Did you even go to that interview I set up for you?"

"Damn! When did you become such a bitch, Deonne!? You're worse than my goddamn mother. If I had known that this is what you would be like, I would never have even moved in!" he lets out a breath of exasperation.

His statement feels like the final nail in the coffin. After all this time, after all I've given, and after all he's taken, he can't even have the decency to be sorry about it. All the hesitation I've been carrying for so long dissipates. This has been a long time coming, I was just too blind to see it.

My fists unclench, I didn't even realize that I was holding on so tightly. Letting out a deep breath, a moment of clarity hits me as I didn't even notice I was in a haze for so long.

"Then why did you even move in with me?" My voice comes out as barely a whisper and that seems to hit him as his features soften.

"Because I love you, Deonne. I'm sorry. I know I made some mistakes but I'm trying. You know it's hard out here, after my boss fired me for no reason–"

That wasn't true...he was fired after going into work late numerous times, and that was if he went at all. When I snap back to focus, it's to catch the end of his spiel:

"--Sure I hit a rough patch, but doesn't everyone? I'm trying! You have to believe me when I say I am trying." He stands up and walks toward me. He grabs my shoulders and Jerome looks at me with the same face that would usually have me crawling back to him. His sad brown eyes always had an effect on me but this time, it just doesn't.

I'm too fed up. Shrugging away from his hold, I step back and wrap my arms around myself.

"I don't, Jerome. I don't believe you even as much as I want to. I just can't anymore."

His face changes way too quickly and the soft expression of remorse and guilt distorts into rage. He grabs the beer bottle, throwing it across the room and it smashes against the wall before falling to the floor in a plethora of broken green shards.

I flinch at the sound as he stomps closer to me, each step he takes I take one back until my back is pressed against the door. He's never hit me-for all the bullshit he put me through that's one thing he never did but with his fists clenched so tightly and his nostrils flaring, I think that he just might.

But I'm not scared. He's taken too much from me.

"What? You think you can just throw me the hell out!? I'm all you have Deonne!" He slams his fist against the wall beside my head. "When everyone leaves you. I'll be the one who's here. I'm it, Deonne. You're not going to get anything better than this. Who else would want you–when you're a four at best! If you don't have me, you're gonna die alone! If you don't have me, you'll have nothing!"

His words hit me like a truck because a part of me actually believes him. That's why I stayed so long but now anything, even if it is nothing, is better than this.

"Well, I don't want this anymore, Jerome. I'm tired. I'm exhausted. If it means I'm gonna die alone, then so be it. I'd rather be alone than be with you any longer." I've never heard myself speak so coldly to him before. But I can see that my words hit him as he takes a step back.

"What? What the hell does that mean?"

I try to ignore the distressed look on his face because if I do I might just take it all back.

"You can't do this to me!--To *us*, Dee. Please don't fucking do this."

Unable to help myself, I look him in the eye one last time.

"I'm sorry Jerome. I really am. *But get the hell out of my house*!"

**Chapter 2**

*His breath feels warm against my skin. It feels soft, like a caress. He runs his hands through my soft coily hair and it sends shivers through me. My breathing becomes erratic and my eyes close. His lips set out to explore every inch of my skin, leaving a trail of wet kisses in their wake, which are like a drug to me.*

*"Mhmhm..." A breathy moan escapes my lips as a shudder ripples through me, he presses soft kisses into my neck. I've never felt this way even with Jerome. It had always been fast and rough and not in a good way but this man, someone I don't know, he takes his time.*

*Pulling away from me, he stares down at me and I finally see his face. Long blonde, nearly-silver hair drapes over his high cheek bones as he looks at me with piercing green eyes so deep it feels like he can see into the depths of my soul. He's so beautiful.*

*"You're so beautiful."*

*He takes the words out of my mouth as he gazes down at me in a way no one has ever looked at me before. Before I can reply, he silences me with his mouth. I feel myself burn with a need so intense that I wrap my arms around his neck and pull him down towards me so his lips meet mine in a fiery kiss.*

*He draws a trail of kisses from my neck, to my jaw, along the curve of my ear, and then down to my collarbone. My core tingles in anticipation as he reaches my navel.*

*Without a warning, he spreads my legs placing his hands on my thighs; he holds them in place and lowers his head. A hot breath of air hits my pussy and I can feel myself dripping in anticipation. His tongue flicks out, sending bolts of lightning as it darts across my insides. Feeling him so close makes me squirm.*

*I expect him to just eat me out and get it over with like how Jerome deals with it but again he takes his sweet time, placing chaste kisses on the insides of my thighs.*

*The man that's on top of me now doesn't seem to have anywhere else he needs to be and has all the time in the world for me as his breathing becomes heavy and he kisses me everywhere but where I want him to.*

*"Please," I moan out before I can stop myself, bucking my hips and wrapping my feet around him in an effort to get his mouth on me where I need it most. He pulls back, leaving me hanging with nothing but air and a thin line of spit to fill the space between us. My body is humming in anticipation and I respond by begging him over and over again, unable to formulate a coherent string of words.*

*His hot breath hits my exposed pussy as he replies, "Please what?" his tone slightly teasing, his hands holding me firmly in place while he looks at me expectantly.*

*His smooth, deep voice sends shivers down my spine.*

*"Please, please." I moan. And the sound of his low chuckle drives me crazy, but before I could finish my sentence, he gives me one deep lick against my pussy. The fire in my core leaps into a full blaze and I can feel myself getting wetter by the second.*

*His tongue is hot as it glides over my flesh and swollen lips. It dips inside me to lap up my juices before he wraps his lips around my clit.*

*As he sucks, one of his hands finds its way to my entrance, he slides a finger into me slowly while his gifted mouth continues teasing me, turning me into a puddle beneath him. My hips move against his mouth but he keeps me in place as I squirm in his hold.*

*Each lick and each thrust of his fingers bring me closer to the edge. The wet sounds of his hungry licking and growls mixed with my breathy moans drive me closer and closer...*

*He inserts another digit inside me, stretching me and I can't help but think of how it would feel once he's inside me. I can feel myself stretching as he explores deeper inside, swirling his finger in a clockwise direction.*

*I grip onto the sheets as I moan louder now, it feels so good I can't stop myself from gasping for air.*

*"Ahhh... please don't stop." I whine, which only makes his movements faster. I feel my orgasm bubbling up inside me as my hips buck against him in desperate need. His hands continue stroking my insides before he grazes his teeth against my throbbing clit and that's all I need.*

*I can't control myself anymore... The wave breaks like an ocean surf crashing down onto the shore...*

*All of my muscles tighten at once and then release. A feeling so powerful flows through every nerve ending in my body as a scream erupts from my throat.*

*"Yes!" I scream and even as my orgasm dies down, he continues to suck, taking in every drop of my cum. He keeps moving his fingers in and out in slow movements.*

*The edges of my mind are foggy now...*

*Lifting his head from in between my legs, he reaches over and runs his fingers through my hair, looking back at me with those piercing green eyes and for a split second; they flash a hot, blood red, his pupils thinning into slits before they return to their emerald green state.*

*I should be scared. But I don't feel any fear except for the anticipation of what he's planning to do to me next. He keeps his gaze on mine as he brings his fingers towards my mouth.*

*"Suck."*

*He commands and normally I wouldn't follow his demand but the desire to please him overtakes me and so I part my lips, allowing him to place his glistening fingers on my tongue.*

*We don't break eye contact as I lick all the cum from his fingers. He lets out a deep breath as I release them from my mouth with a pop.*

*"I want you inside me."*

*The orgasm he just gave me isn't enough. I want more. I can't help but want more.*

*He smirks at me. "Do you now?"*

*I nod, breathless.*

*"Your wish is my command."*

*Moving so smoothly that it almost seems inhuman, he nestles himself in between my legs, staring down at me with a look of lust and need. The air sizzles like someone took a hot iron to it as his cock pushes up against my opening from underneath. I wait for him to ease himself into me but instead he slams against me.*

*"Ah!" I gasp sharply at the sudden but welcomed intrusion. He fills me up, stretching me to the point that it's almost painful.*

*He pauses for a second, watching my reaction as he pulls out before pushing himself back in, causing my toes to curl again at the feeling that's building up in my belly once more. As he thrusts into me, my walls grip onto him, almost afraid to let him go. I can feel myself stretch around him. His body is tight against mine and his muscles move like a well-oiled machine.*

*"Who do you belong to?"He asks, keeping himself steady yet deep inside me. I move my hips but he halts my movement, wrapping his fingers around my throat.*

*"I said who do you belong to?" He repeats, his voice almost like a growl as his hold tightens at the base of my throat but doesn't suffocate me. His hold is solid and strong, but not painful. He rocks his hips and I'm forced to move with him or fall away.*

*In a haze of want, I answer: "I'm yours." My voice claws out of my throat, my words barely audible but I hope he understands.*

*He smiles and it takes my breath away.*

*I've never seen someone smile so beautifully before that I can't help but repeat;*

*"I'm all yours."*

"I'm all yours," I say in a listless murmur as I slowly come awake, but when I open my eyes again, he's gone. I jolt up in bed.

The sun's just starting to rise and the first bit of golden light peeks through the blinds.

There's a moment of disorientation as I try to figure out what just happened. Looking beside me, I expect the green-eyed man to be there but it's empty.

Throwing the quilted coverlet off of myself, I can see the evidence of what happened. There's a damp spot in the sheets below, and I can feel myself blushing as I realize that I must have had one of the most intense wet dreams of my life.

I touch my fingers to my full lips, still feeling the phantom sensation of his mouth on mine.

I close my eyes and try to will the handsome stranger back to me but he's gone. It was just a dream.

A beautiful, amazing dream.

It was so strange since my dreams were rarely so vivid, in fact, normally I hardly ever remembered them at all.

And then, everything that just happened the night before comes rushing back.

Jerome is gone. Freedom has never felt so good before but I still can't shake the feeling of his loss.

"God, it was all just a dream." I sink back down in my bed. It had felt all too real. Even now, I can still feel the cum soaking my panties.

Sleeping has always been a bit hard for me. I've always been restless, and sleeping beside Jerome certainly didn't help things but today I feel refreshed.

I also still feel stretched, like my dream lover's dick was actually inside me. I can still feel his touch on my skin, his soft lips. My body is sticky with sweat and cum and my hair's a tangled mess. It was so real that I can't help but wonder if he was really here or not. Maybe this is just a sign that I need to get laid because, to be frank, Jerome wasn't good at a lot of things, and that included sex.

Getting out of bed, I let out a deep sigh. If only men like that actually existed, like the one in my dreams. How could someone be so beautiful and gentle yet rough in all the right ways?

Walking toward my window, I let out a deep sigh and open the blinds so I can look out into the world, and I am greeted by the stillness of dawn. The sky is streaked with pink, blue, and orange, and the sun dominates half of the horizon with its cheerful warmth. My mind is still playing vivid flashbacks from last night when I realize:

"I didn't even get to cum with his dick!"

*His breath feels warm against my skin. It feels soft, like a caress. He runs his hands through my soft coily hair and it sends shivers through me. My breathing becomes erratic and my eyes close. His lips set out to explore every inch of my skin, leaving a trail of wet kisses in their wake, which are like a drug to me.*

*"Mhmhm..." A breathy moan escapes my lips as a shudder ripples through me, he presses soft kisses into my neck. I've never felt this way even with Jerome. It had always been fast and rough and not in a good way but this man, someone I don't know, he takes his time.*

*Pulling away from me, he stares down at me and I finally see his face. Long blonde, nearly-silver hair drapes over his high cheek bones as he looks at me with piercing green eyes so deep it feels like he can see into the depths of my soul. He's so beautiful.*

*"You're so beautiful."*

*He takes the words out of my mouth as he gazes down at me in a way no one has ever looked at me before. Before I can reply, he silences me with his mouth. I feel myself burn with a need so intense that I wrap my arms around his neck and pull him down towards me so his lips meet mine in a fiery kiss.*

*He draws a trail of kisses from my neck, to my jaw, along the curve of my ear, and then down to my collarbone. My core tingles in anticipation as he reaches my navel.*

*Without a warning, he spreads my legs placing his hands on my thighs; he holds them in place and lowers his head. A hot breath of air hits my pussy and I can feel myself dripping in anticipation. His tongue flicks out, sending bolts of lightning as it darts across my insides. Feeling him so close makes me squirm.*

*I expect him to just eat me out and get it over with like how Jerome deals with it but again he takes his sweet time, placing chaste kisses on the insides of my thighs.*

*The man that's on top of me now doesn't seem to have anywhere else he needs to be and has all the time in the world for me as his breathing becomes heavy and he kisses me everywhere but where I want him to.*

*"Please," I moan out before I can stop myself, bucking my hips and wrapping my feet around him in an effort to get his mouth on me where I need it most. He pulls back, leaving me hanging with nothing but air and a thin line of spit to fill the space between us. My body is humming in anticipation and I respond by begging him over and over again, unable to formulate a coherent string of words.*

*His hot breath hits my exposed pussy as he replies, "Please what?" his tone slightly teasing, his hands holding me firmly in place while he looks at me expectantly.*

*His smooth, deep voice sends shivers down my spine.*

*"Please, please." I moan. And the sound of his low chuckle drives me crazy, but before I could finish my sentence, he gives me one deep lick against my pussy. The fire in my core leaps into a full blaze and I can feel myself getting wetter by the second.*

*His tongue is hot as it glides over my flesh and swollen lips. It dips inside me to lap up my juices before he wraps his lips around my clit.*
*As he sucks, one of his hands finds its way to my entrance, he slides a finger into me slowly while his gifted mouth continues teasing me, turning me into a puddle beneath him. My hips move against his mouth but he keeps me in place as I squirm in his hold.*
*Each lick and each thrust of his fingers bring me closer to the edge. The wet sounds of his hungry licking and growls mixed with my breathy moans drive me closer and closer...*
*He inserts another digit inside me, stretching me and I can't help but think of how it would feel once he's inside me. I can feel myself stretching as he explores deeper inside, swirling his finger in a clockwise direction. I grip onto the sheets as I moan louder now, it feels so good I can't stop myself from gasping for air.*
*"Ahhh... please don't stop." I whine, which only makes his movements faster. I feel my orgasm bubbling up inside me as my hips buck against him in desperate need. His hands continue stroking my insides before he grazes his teeth against my throbbing clit and that's all I need.*
*I can't control myself anymore... The wave breaks like an ocean surf crashing down onto the shore...*
*All of my muscles tighten at once and then release. A feeling so powerful flows through every nerve ending in my body as a scream erupts from my throat.*
*"Yes!" I scream and even as my orgasm dies down, he continues to suck, taking in every drop of my cum. He keeps moving his fingers in and out in slow movements.*
*The edges of my mind are foggy now...*
*Lifting his head from in between my legs, he reaches over and runs his fingers through my hair, looking back at me with those piercing green*

*eyes and for a split second; they flash a hot, blood red, his pupils thinning into slits before they return to their emerald green state.*

*I should be scared. But I don't feel any fear except for the anticipation of what he's planning to do to me next. He keeps his gaze on mine as he brings his fingers towards my mouth.*

*"Suck."*

*He commands and normally I wouldn't follow his demand but the desire to please him overtakes me and so I part my lips, allowing him to place his glistening fingers on my tongue.*

*We don't break eye contact as I lick all the cum from his fingers. He lets out a deep breath as I release them from my mouth with a pop.*

*"I want you inside me."*

*The orgasm he just gave me isn't enough. I want more. I can't help but want more.*

*He smirks at me. "Do you now?"*

*I nod, breathless.*

*"Your wish is my command."*

*Moving so smoothly that it almost seems inhuman, he nestles himself in between my legs, staring down at me with a look of lust and need. The air sizzles like someone took a hot iron to it as his cock pushes up against my opening from underneath. I wait for him to ease himself into me but instead he slams against me.*

*"Ah!" I gasp sharply at the sudden but welcomed intrusion. He fills me up, stretching me to the point that it's almost painful.*

*He pauses for a second, watching my reaction as he pulls out before pushing himself back in, causing my toes to curl again at the feeling that's building up in my belly once more. As he thrusts into me, my walls grip onto him, almost afraid to let him go. I can feel myself stretch around him. His body is tight against mine and his muscles move like a well-oiled machine.*

*"Who do you belong to?"He asks, keeping himself steady yet deep inside me. I move my hips but he halts my movement, wrapping his fingers around my throat.*

*"I said who do you belong to?" He repeats, his voice almost like a growl as his hold tightens at the base of my throat but doesn't suffocate me. His hold is solid and strong, but not painful. He rocks his hips and I'm forced to move with him or fall away.*

*In a haze of want, I answer: "I'm yours." My voice claws out of my throat, my words barely audible but I hope he understands.*

*He smiles and it takes my breath away.*

*I've never seen someone smile so beautifully before that I can't help but repeat;*

*"I'm all yours."*

"I'm all yours," I say in a listless murmur as I slowly come awake, but when I open my eyes again, he's gone. I jolt up in bed.

The sun's just starting to rise and the first bit of golden light peeks through the blinds.

There's a moment of disorientation as I try to figure out what just happened. Looking beside me, I expect the green-eyed man to be there but it's empty.

Throwing the quilted coverlet off of myself, I can see the evidence of what happened. There's a damp spot in the sheets below, and I can feel myself blushing as I realize that I must have had one of the most intense wet dreams of my life.

I touch my fingers to my full lips, still feeling the phantom sensation of his mouth on mine.

I close my eyes and try to will the handsome stranger back to me but he's gone. It was just a dream.

A beautiful, amazing dream.

It was so strange since my dreams were rarely so vivid, in fact, normally I hardly ever remembered them at all.

And then, everything that just happened the night before comes rushing back.

Jerome is gone. Freedom has never felt so good before but I still can't shake the feeling of his loss.

"God, it was all just a dream." I sink back down in my bed. It had felt all too real. Even now, I can still feel the cum soaking my panties.

Sleeping has always been a bit hard for me. I've always been restless, and sleeping beside Jerome certainly didn't help things but today I feel refreshed.

I also still feel stretched, like my dream lover's dick was actually inside me. I can still feel his touch on my skin, his soft lips. My body is sticky with sweat and cum and my hair's a tangled mess. It was so real that I can't help but wonder if he was really here or not. Maybe this is just a sign that I need to get laid because, to be frank, Jerome wasn't good at a lot of things, and that included sex.

Getting out of bed, I let out a deep sigh. If only men like that actually existed, like the one in my dreams. How could someone be so beautiful and gentle yet rough in all the right ways?

Walking toward my window, I let out a deep sigh and open the blinds so I can look out into the world, and I am greeted by the stillness of dawn. The sky is streaked with pink, blue, and orange, and the sun dominates half of the horizon with its cheerful warmth. My mind is still playing vivid flashbacks from last night when I realize:

"I didn't even get to cum with his dick!"

**To be continued...**

**Read the rest of this steamy romance by purchasing *WET DREAM***

Made in the USA
Columbia, SC
06 June 2024

36703327R00089